Weathering the
STORMS

Weathering the STORMS

Terry Webb

Pleasant Word

Pleasant Word (a division of WinePress Publishing, PO Box 428, Enumclaw, WA 98022) functions only as book publisher. As such, the ultimate design, content, editorial accuracy, and views expressed or implied in this work are those of the author.

Unless otherwise noted, all Scriptures are taken from the Holy Bible, New International Version, Copyright © 1973, 1978, 1984 by the International Bible Society. Used by permission of Zondervan Publishing House. The "NIV" and "New International Version" trademarks are registered in the United States Patent and Trademark Office by International Bible Society.

ISBN 1-4141-0393-X
Library of Congress Catalog Card Number: 2005900979

Dedication

This story is dedicated to:

Matthew and Billy, 13-years-old at this writing, and Rachel, for her dramatic reading the summer of 2004.

Table of Contents

Acknowledgment

I wish to acknowledge that my retelling of the First World Series games in 1903 came primarily from the accounts of those games recorded in Louis Masur's book, *Autumn Glory* (Hill and Wang, New York, 2003). I also want to thank Loretta Bradley for sharing the story with me of Captain Josiah Mitchell's longboat journey from the *Hornet* to Hawaii in 1866. This classic tale of survival at sea inspired the events in this fictional story. The brave members of the New England Lighthouse Lovers, who surviving the storm on Nantucket in 2005, were with me in spirit while I finished writing this book. Last but not least, I owe a huge debt of gratitude to Carolyn Yoder, my editor at the Chautauqua 2004 Highlights Foundation Writers Workshop, who lovingly critiqued the manuscript.

CHAPTER 1

Calm Before Storms

September 3, 1903: Winds SW 0-5. Sunny.
No ships in sight except Rainbow.

—Louie Hollander

Summer Doldrums, Ma called the weather.

Usually comes before a storm, she told Louie that morning. September storms—Louie remembered how fierce they could be.

"Eerie," Louie added.

After morning chores he'd taken his pocketknife and found just the right stick of driftwood to whittle. He'd milked the cow and fed the chickens but hadn't caught a fish. He dreaded the thought of canned beans for dinner again but the fish just weren't biting in this heat.

"Irascible rocks!" He mumbled.

Several times Louie changed rocks to find a more comfortable sitting position.

"Too lumpy," he added, bending over the obstinate object in his hands. He brushed away a lock of bushy hair over his eyes with his arm and wiped his sweaty hands on his shirt.

Louie whittled away at the knot in the driftwood until a beak formed. He carefully closed his new pocketknife and placed it down beside him. *Wish I could run—anywhere—around bases or up and down grassy slopes*, he thought to himself, *or even jump off the rock ledge into the icy cold ocean water.* Instead, he stood up and with a two-step jumped over a nearby crevice to the next big rock. Lifting his arms for balance, he climbed up and over the rocks that made up most of the surface of the two-acre island. After two months on Two Tree Island, Louie had mastered and memorized all the rocks—just as he had the ships that passed the island on regular runs.

Besides all his other chores, Louie conducted tours when summer folk brought their families to visit the lighthouse. For the past week there had been no visitors—nor had the familiar summer pleasure vessels passed by. Each day had dawned bright and clear—and still.

Ma appeared at his side and pointed to the placid sea.

"Not a breath of air anywhere," she said.

Louie felt as languid as the sea. He turned to Ma.

"I'm bored. There's no one around to play with. Charlie's gone home. Sammy's gone, too—at least most of the time—except when I'm lighting the lamp beacon. Sometimes he comes back to sit on the tower railing. He 'kuk kuks,' then flies away to be with the other seagulls. I don't have any friends anymore. I need another pet."

"There's Betsy, our cow, and the chickens," Ma replied.

"But they're not pets," Louie said.

"If you're bored, how about collecting some of that moss over there for me? With this bright sun it ought to bleach fast—then we can make some sea moss pudding. You can start by picking out the weeds and seaweed and then spreading the moss on level rocks. Should be good drying weather since there is no rain in sight. Then pick us some blueberries for dinner."

Louie moaned and muttered under this breath, "Just like Ma to give me something to do. Don't mothers ever understand? I wish Charlie were still visiting or at least Uncle Sam. I haven't seen either of them for a week. I can't even look forward to going back to school like Charlie."

His thoughts rambled on. *Since Uncle Sam was only a visiting summer preacher, I probably won't ever see him again.*

Louie pulled some of the gray-green moss off the rock nearest him and picked out the seaweed. With a wide sweep he threw the seaweed toward the open ocean. Then he laid the moss out on a flat, bare rock to dry. As he did so, he spied some luscious-looking blueberries, partly hidden under some nearby bushes. He picked some of the little dark blue ones, leaving the green ones. He ate some and put a few in his overall pockets. Intent on finding as many blueberries as he could underneath the low-lying branches Louie never heard the dory approach.

Captain Bowline's familiar voice booming over the water startled him.

"Ahoy, mate!"

Louie turned around, pocketing the last berry as he leapt over rocks to reach the dory before she landed.

Captain Bowline waved an envelope.

"Thought ye'd like this here letter. Postman gave it to me 'afore I left. Looks like your friend Charlie writ'n you." He handed the envelope to Louie.

"I'll be a'visit'n with yer ma."

Captain Bowline turned and headed back up to the house while Louie eagerly tore open the envelope. Several penciled pages fell out. He grabbed one and read,

Dear Louie,

How 'ya do'n?

Louie could almost hear Charlie's raspy voice. He read and reread the letter. He had been worried about Charlie—going back home to such a mean pa who hit his ma, Charlie, and his sister, Lucy, whenever he came home drunk.

> The whole fishing fleet left yesterday to catch cod off the Banks. Ben went with Pa on the *Tipsy*. I tried to convince Pa to take me, too, but Ma said I had to stay home 'cause of school. Ben gave me that evil eye look, then mumbled "You ain't old enough." Ben's in charge of one of them dories and you'd think he was the captain instead of Pa. Ma also said I'd miss baseball practices then coach would kick me off the team. Wish you were here so's we could talk.
>
> Here's cross hand'n ye.
>
> —Charlie

With Charlie's letter in hand, Louie skipped up the hill to join Ma and Captain Bowline in the kitchen.

"She's going to the Grand Banks!" He announced.

"Who's going?" Ma answered.

"Don't you remember, Ma? The *Tipsy* joins the fishing fleet in the fall and spring to fish the Grand Banks near Nova Scotia."

Louie had seen the fleet off with Charlie when they lived at Swanton Point. Each schooner carried about five dories on each side of the ship. When they reached the fishing waters, these dories would set off from the mother ship with a tub trawl.[1] Leaving a floating barrel at one end of the line each dory would row downwind paying out the hooked line, waiting for the big fish to bite. Louie knew how dangerous the work was, especially in rough seas.

"Boy, am I glad Charlie wasn't allowed to go because I don't want to lose him." Louie knew that sailors' lives had been lost and dories overturned in rough waters.

Charlie had a widow's walk[2] on top of his house. When Louie lived near Charlie at Swanton Point, he had often waited and watched for the *Tipsy* and the other schooners to come into port from that walk.

"Ma, please can I go visit Charlie? There's nothing much to do here in the doldrums anyway."

"Maybe. We'll see. Maybe during our time off." Ma answered.

"And when's that going to be? We're stuck here on this island..."

"I was a' thinking," Captain Bowline interrupted. He was seated at the table enjoying one of Ma's biscuits and coffee, "Maybe ye'd like to see our new pups. Our Newfoundland Sally's just had her first littah." And turning to Louie's ma he added, "Think you could manage while I whisk Louie back to town for a spell?"

"Could I, Ma?"

Ma looked at Louie sternly. "Hurry along now with Captain Bowline. But remember—puppies and islands don't mix."

---

[1] The trawl, or 1½ mile long rope with hooks fastened every 9 feet on three foot pieces of line, was stored in a wooden tub.

[2] A fenced-in place on top of the flat part of the roof.

CHAPTER 2

Playful Pups

How many, Cap'n?"

Louie said as he jumped into the dory after winching it down from the slip.

"Six," the Captain answered as he rowed the dory away from the shore toward the *Rainbow*. He tied up the dory to the stern cleat and they both climbed on board.

Louie helped the Captain weigh anchor.[3] The make n' break engine[4] coughed, sputtered, coughed again, and then turned over.

Captain Bowline turned *Rainbow's* bow toward port. Two Tree Island disappeared behind the moving ship.

Sure beats boredom, Louie thought to himself. The adrenalin rushed through his veins as the *Rainbow* picked up speed. *We're moving! At last I'll have a chance to stretch my legs in a civilized place rather than sitting alone on a rock pile with just Ma to bug me.*

He took a long deep breath of the salty air. The town wharf came into view with its long pier and shack sitting in the middle of it. A path led to gray-shingled buildings that dotted the sloping hillside behind the shack as far as he could see.

When Captain Bowline spoke again, he said, "Prepare to dock."

Louie put the bumpers over the side of the boat nearest the float.[5] He held the painter[6] and made ready to jump off and cleat[7] her as she came alongside. Captain Bowline shut off the engine and cleated the stern line with his favorite knot. Louie jumped out of the dory, shook out his sea legs, and touched some of the colorful lobster buoys that hung from nails helter-skelter from the side of the boathouse. He kicked over a lobster trap and it clattered off the side of the pier, landing on the rocks.

"Watch where you be walk'n, now." Captain Bowline reminded him.

At the end of the narrow pathway leading into town, some of the buildings met each other. These framed the main street of the town. Most of the other buildings faced the water except for those that bordered this street. Louie read the billboards as he started walking down the Street. One advertised the popular soda drink, *Moxie*. In addition to Jake's store—that Louie knew contained everything anyone would need—he noted signs for a US Post Office, a Barber Shop, and a Blacksmith Shop.

"Must stop at Jake's with yer Ma's grocery list 'a fore we return you to Two Tree Island," Captain Bowline said on their way past the all-goods store.

"And don't forget to buy some *Moxies*," Louie added. His mouth watered and he could almost taste his favorite refreshing drink.

A group of boys walked passed Louie. They giggled and pointed to his worn out old clothes. Louie looked down at his patched overalls and felt out of place. He tried to smile back at the boys but the smile froze before it formed.

"Guess I need to get one of the caps they're wearing and remind Ma to buy me those new clothes she promised," he mumbled to himself.

They passed the town boarding house where he and Ma had stayed when he had gone with Ma to apply for the job as the lighthouse keeper for the island light. Some old women sitting in rocking chairs knitting on the wide piazza looked up and grinned at both of them.

"How you been, Cap'n?" one of them asked. "Who's that young'n with you?"

Captain Bowline tipped his hat. "Never been bettah. This here's Louie Hollandah. He and his ma tend Two Tree Island Light yonder."

"Good afternoon Ma'am." Louie took his cap off and held it under his arm. He shook hands with each of the women. He now remembered how most town folks were friendly. He tried to forget about the boys' jeers and think about the puppies he would soon hold.

Louie walked with Captain Bowline up a hill along one of the winding footpaths toward a weathered white clapboard house with a wide sloping roof facing the water. Glass framed the top and sides of a big front door. Large glass windows with half-pulled shades were like two eyes blinking at him. Mrs. Bowline stood at the open door wiping her hands on her apron.

"Tommy's out back with Sally and her pups. Bet yer dying to see 'em."

"Am I ever, thanks…." Louie's words trailed off. He was already on his way to the fenced-in yard behind the house. Eight-year-old Tommy had become like a younger brother to him. Louie waved at Tommy when he saw him. Tommy held up a black and white puppy.

"This one's the runt—but I like him the best. Open the gate quickly and slip in before the other puppies get out."

Before Louie could get the gate latched behind him, three small balls of fur were on his feet, chewing on his bootlaces. He bent down and picked them all up in his arms. They had long floppy ears and pug nose faces. The puppies nuzzled his neck and licked his face.

"You're cute," he said contentedly.

"Where are the other two pups?" Louie asked Tommy.

"They've dug a hole under the porch and like to hide there."

Tommy went over to the porch and crawled part way underneath to pull out two more puppies, their noses covered with mud. One was so dirty you could barely tell she had white on her. The other was all black.

"Which puppy do you like?" Tommy asked Louie. "Ma and Pa said you could have first pick after they're weaned and every lighthouse needs a Newfoundland dog."

Louie's heart melted at the thought that one of these adorable pups might be—could be—his. He yearned for a new pet to take care of, to play with, to be his pal. But Ma…his thoughts trailed off—*would she let him have a dog on the island?* Ma might not even consider the idea. If she agreed to any dog he thought it might be a hard sell.

"I like them all," he sighed.

As if he could read Louie's thoughts, Captain Bowline, who had by then joined them in the yard, said, "Don't worry, Louie, I'll help ye convince yer ma. But if I don't get ye back 'afore nightfall to tend that light beacon, we'll both be in a peck of trouble."

"I'll go on ahead and get your Ma's victuals[8] whilst you decide," Captain Bowline said.

"I guess if I have to pick one…" Louie picked up each puppy one by one.

He held the black one with white spots on her ears the longest. She still had mud on her nose. With a "woof" she burrowed under his arm.

"…this will be the one."

Louie put her down gently beside the others who had gone back to Sally pushing and shoving each other to reach their nourishment.

The puppy tugged at his heartstrings as he reluctantly said goodbye and turned toward town. He wanted to take her with him.

In the distance Louie spied a figure nearing the town wharf carrying a box. Could that be Captain Bowline? He sprinted the rest of the way. Sure enough Captain Bowline was stowing[9] the box with the groceries when he reached him.

"Make ready to cast off. We've no time to lose."

The yellow ball of fire darted in and out behind the wisps of clouds on the western horizon. The setting sun reminded Louie of the diminutive ball of fur that had tried to hide under the Bowline's porch and under Louie's arm. Now he had to think of a way to convince Ma that they needed a dog on Two Tree Island.

The *Rainbow* anchored off the lee side of the island. Louie rowed the dory into the landing place where Ma waited to winch her up the slip.

"No time to waste, sun's ready to set," she said to Louie.

"Here, don't forget yer *Moxie*." Captain Bowline handed Louie a bottle.

"Thanks."

Louie drank some of the refreshing drink, and then wedged the bottle between two rocks as he pushed off the dory. He finished the *Moxie* and began his climb back up to the house carrying the box of groceries. His heart beat fast and his hands were clammy. He turned his head and said to Ma, who was following him up the hill, "Got something to tell—I mean ask—you."

He was thinking about how to convince her that they needed a dog as he climbed the steps of the lighthouse tower, poured kerosene into the lamp jet reservoir, and lit the wick. He thought about the puppy when he opened the logbook and wrote the account of that day. Having a dog for a friend would make life so much more exciting on this island.

September 3 (con't) Went to town with Captain Bowline on the Rainbow. Light variable winds.
Bowlines have six Newfoundland puppies.

—Louie Hollander

---

[3] Breaking and lifting an anchor off the seabed.

[4] Type of marine engine.

[5] A floating dock, connected to a gangway that moves up and down with the tides.

[6] The rope on the bow of the boat.

[7] Tying ropes to a wood or metal fastener with two arms.

[8] Food supplies.

[9] Putting away.

CHAPTER 3

Convincing Ma

R emember Milo?"

Louie asked Ma when he sat down to eat.

Ma had made clam chowder for supper. Louie slurped a spoonful and then took a bite of brown bread. He waited for Ma to reply.

"Milo? Oh you mean the dog in the painting at Swanton Point?" Ma queried. "Did the puppies you saw at the Bowlines' house look like him?"

"Sort-of. Only they were cuter."

"Of course they were cuter; they're only puppies. But puppies grow up to be dogs."

"Newfoundland dogs, like Milo. Remember that painting called *Saved*? Milo became famous because he swam after a loon at Egg Rock Light. He even saved two children from drowning."

Now, he'd said it. He watched Ma's face for a hint of what she would say.

Her lips pursed together and she put up her hand like a stop sign.

"Louie, we don't need a dog like Milo when we have a hen, a rooster, chickens, and a cow on this island. A dog would only cause trouble."

Louie took a deep breath and then went on.

"Newfoundland dogs make great pets, Ma. And sometimes..." Louie went on, "Newfoundland dogs rescue boats and people. A dog would be a big help on this island. Besides, I don't have a pet anymore. Since Sammy's wing has mended, he's with the other seagulls most of the time. Please, Ma?"

Louie stopped for another breath. He waited for her reply.

"Just who is going to take care of training this puppy you want so badly?"

"I will!" Louie nearly burst. "Can I Ma? I mean can we have one of the Bowline puppies? The Bowlines said I could have the first pick of the litter when they're weaned. They even said that we should have a Newfoundland dog—that every lighthouse needs one."

"We'll see. I'll have to talk to the Bowlines first before I decide. Now..." Ma reached in the box of groceries and pulled out some magazines. "I asked Captain Bowline to buy the newest issues of *Boy's Life* magazine. Thought you'd like something new to read."

"Thanks, Ma!"

Louie gave Ma a peck on the cheek and climbed the stairs to the loft with his new magazines under his arm. He no longer worried about how he could convince Ma to take one of the Bowline's puppies. Her "We'll see" usually meant "yes".

He looked at some of the ads in the newest issue of *Boy's Life*. Louie especially liked the box camera ad. He wished he'd had one of those to take a flash photo of the puppies. He read the second installment of the biography of Robert Lewis Stevenson before extinguishing the wick on the kerosene lantern beside his bed. Tomorrow would be more lighthouse chores to do and he'd have to get up earlier to try and catch a fish.

CHAPTER 4

Coal and Books

September 9, 1903. Cloudy. Southwest Wind 5-15.
Coal gundalow arrives with winter supply. Put coal in
old boat shed. Lighthouse tender brings Mr. McAllister,
Miss Gilbert, and schoolbooks.

—Louie Hollander

A mysterious ship broke through the morning mist.

Louie looked up as he was taking the wiggly mackerel he'd just caught off the hook. Strange—no sails up, almost like a ghost ship. A shiver ran up Louie's spine. *Did she come up from the briny deep?* Louie wondered. She was so low in the water.

The apparition that appeared out of the mist was a low flat boat with square ends. That must be the gundalow[10] bringing coal. Mr. McAllister had told them to be expecting it any day.

He called to Ma as he took the steps two by two with the fish thrashing in a bucket.

"Come see—we have visitors. How do you suppose that gundalow got here? Sure couldn't sail by herself when there's hardly any breath of air. Must have an engine somewhere to give her a push. Good thing the sea is calm today—that boat—if you could call it that—just might capsize in a rough sea."

Ma came down the steps behind Louie singing.

"Gundalow roll, gundalow sail. Carry the lumber, the coal and the mail."[11]

Louie could hear the motor as the scow drew near the wharf. Then he saw that the sails were furled onto the strange mast. A sailor threw some lines and Louie made them fast.

"Morn'n, " one sailor said. "Think you can give us a hand with this here coal? Where's yer coal shed?"

"Over there—our old boat house." Louie pointed to the shed at the top of the ramp.

"Glad we brought the bucket. Can you help us hitch her to the pulley after we load her?" The men placed a bucket cart on the wharf and started shoveling coal into it.

Louie was glad that it was high tide. The work was hard enough without having to lift the coal up any higher.

After loading the cart two of the sailors pushed it over to the slip, the ramp leading to the shed. Louie hitched the cart to the chain and pulled it up the ramp. Then he helped the men unload the coal.

Louie coughed. Coal dust was everywhere—even in his lungs. But they couldn't stop working until the shed was full.

As the sun rose in the sky, the sea fell below the wharf. Louie warned the sailors that they might find the gundalow stuck on rocks if they didn't leave before the tide had completely ebbed.

No sooner had Louie gotten back up to the house and cleaned up when a low horn blast announced another boat arriving.

"Oh no!" said Louie, "It couldn't be the inspector again. He was just here."

He climbed the tower steps to see who was arriving. It looked like the lighthouse tender all right. Louie panicked as he thought of all the cleaning that still needed doing. At least they've anchored on the lee side of the island, giving him more time to get the lighthouse ready. He grabbed a wiping cloth with one hand and started polishing the lenses. Then he looked through the spyglass again and saw that there were two figures in the dory with a seaman rowing. One was a tall woman wearing a bonnet. She didn't look familiar. He finally recognized Mr. McAllister and breathed a sigh of relief. He climbed back down the winding steps and headed to the landing slip.

"Like you to meet Miss Gilbert," Mr. McAllister said as the dory slid into the slip.

He helped the tall woman step out onto a rock. Louie noted that she held her head erect. He watched curiously as she gathered her skirts and petticoat in one hand and stepped jauntily out onto the rocks adjusting her shawl as she did so.

"She's going to be yer teachah for school'n," Mr. McAllister added.

Before reaching out his hand to shake the one the teacher held out to him, Louie noted that wisps of gray hair stuck out from under her bonnet and her face was wrinkled. Louie wasn't sure he wanted this ancient lady for his schoolteacher.

Remembering his manners, he took her hand and said.

"Good day, Ma'am. Glad to meet you."

"Got a big box of school books for ye, too," Mr. McAllister added.

The seaman took a square tin box out of the dory. Louie helped him carry the box up to the house where Ma was waiting.

"Just put it over there in the parlor," Ma said to the seaman. She turned to greet Miss Gilbert and Mr. McAllister.

------

[10] a type of barge that carried freight.
[11] "The Gundalow Song," Words & Music by The Shaw Brothers.

CHAPTER 5

School on Rocks

L et's see what's in this box."

Miss Gilbert settled herself on the stiff backed sofa in the parlor. She lifted out the first book.

"The Ladies Auxiliary prepares the boxes for me to take around to all the inhabited islands around this bay. I never know what's going to be in the boxes. Now look here—what is a grown boy like you going to do with a McGuffey Primer!" She put the book aside and took out another.

"Holman Day's *Pine Tree Ballads: Rhymed Stories of Unplanned Human Natur' up in Maine*. She's a good poet. We can use this one."

Louie smiled. Miss Gilbert just might be all right. He liked poetry and had written poems about birds in his old school.

Louie reached over and took out the next one. Thomas Harvey's *Practical Grammar of the English Language*. He made a face. He hated grammar.

Miss Gilbert saw the face and said, "Well, might come in handy when you write, so let's keep it. Sort of like Webster's Dictionary."

Which was the next book she took out of the box. There were only a few left now. Louie could see some composition books, a compass, some lead pencils with rubber tips, a pen, some Carter's ink and a penholder around the side of the box.

"Now here's one I think I'll take back with the primer, Welsh's *A New System of Mercantile Arithmetick*, published in 1812. Did the ladies think you're going to sell cloth from an island lighthouse?"

Louie laughed.

The two books left were Scott's *A School History of the US* and Buckley's *A Short History of Natural Science and the Progress of Discovery*.

"These will have to do until I can find out what grade you finished last year so I can bring the right books. What grade did you finish?"

"Eighth grade. That's the grade I was in at Swanton Point. But I didn't learn much the last half of the year because my pa died and ...."

"I'm sorry to hear that," interrupted Miss Gilbert, "must have been awful for you losing your pa."

Louie winced. "Yes, it was."

He turned his face away to wipe a tear from the corner of his eye. Boys weren't supposed to cry. But he couldn't help it when someone reminded him about losing Pa.

"Well, we'll start with lessons from the end of eighth grade—just to catch you up. Were you studying geometry?"

Louie nodded his head.

"Then we'll have to find an eighth grade geometry book. What books do you like to read?"

Louie told her that he liked Mark Twain and had read all of *Tom Sawyer* and *Huckleberry Finn*. Miss Gilbert promised she'd bring another of Mark Twain's books with her when she came back.

"Now, let's start you on the first two chapters of the *Natural History* book."

She took out the composition book and wrote down Louie's lessons for the next two weeks then read them to him and asked if he had any questions.

Louie overheard Ma and Mr. McAllister talking and laughing in the kitchen.

A vision of Ma and Pa talking and laughing together in the kitchen at Swanton Point popped into his head. But the man's voice he heard wasn't Pa's. It was Mr. McAllister's. Mr. McAllister used to call him boy. He hadn't liked him then and didn't like him talking to Ma. Anger welled up in Louie's throat and he clenched his fists.

What business did Mr. McAllister have talking and laughing with Ma like Pa used to do! Louie couldn't concentrate on what Miss Gilbert was saying. Visions of Ma and Pa talking and laughing in the kitchen together at Swanton Point crowded his head.

"What?" he turned to Miss Gilbert.

"Do you have any questions?" She asked again.

"No thanks. I think I can manage."

Just then Ma came around the corner.

"Ready to join us for dinner?"

Later that afternoon, after Miss Gilbert and Mr. McAllister left and Louie and Ma were preparing the lighthouse for the night vigil, Louie turned to her and said.

"I don't like you spending so much time with that Mr. McAllister."

"So much time? How often do we have visitors, Louie? We need to be sociable when they come."

Louie scowled at Ma. She kept on washing the dishes.

"I don't like you being sociable with him!" Louie shouted.

"Can I see one of your new books?" Ma asked.

Louie shoved *The Pine Tree Ballads* under her nose, then he grabbed it back and stomped up the loft steps. Reading one of the ballads relaxed the nagging meanness he felt in his muscles.

CHAPTER 6

Welcome Arrivals

S ome days he just fell into bed bone weary.

The past week had gone by quickly with school lessons to add to the usual daily routine. As Louie milked Betsy, collected eggs, and tended the light beacon, he thought of the puppy he wanted so badly. When he carried buckets of coal up the hill, he heard a whining. Was it his puppy crying for him? No, just the wind whistling.

In addition to her lighthouse chores, cooking, and cleaning, Ma had put up jars of blueberry and raspberry jam. Even then it seemed to Louie Ma was after him every free minute.

"Have you done your lessons?"

Now it was Monday morning, and Louie was studying the natural history book Miss Gilbert had brought. He was thinking of a word to describe what lichens, leeches, and barnacles have in common when he saw the *Rainbow* dropping anchor. He put the book aside and met the dory at the landing site.

Louie saw the Captain and Mrs. Bowline first. And he ran into the water—shoes and all—when he saw Uncle Sam Hornblower seated in the stern seat beside Tommy. He gave him a big bear hug nearly capsizing the dory as he did so.

"Hey! How 'bout hitching us 'afore we capsize," Captain Bowline growled. He jumped out of the dory and grabbed the gunwales to steady the boat. Louie sloshed back to the bow and hitched the chain. When he came back to the dory to help Mrs. Bowline disembark, he noted the bundle in Tommy's lap.

"What's that?" he asked.

"Yer pup."

Louie took the bundle eagerly from Tommy's outstretched hands. He rubbed the soft canine head that peeked out and licked his face. "Woof," she said.

Uncle Sam helped Mrs. Bowline carry the boxes and bags of food she had brought. "Thought yer Ma would like some of these fresh veg'tables from our garden—tomatoes, corn, and squash. Got to eat 'em 'afore the frost hits."

"Corn on the cob," Louie said, "I haven't had any since Swanton Point."

"Did ye convince yer Ma, 'bout this here pup?" Captain Bowline asked. "'Cause if ye didn't we're here to help ye. He's a right cute fellah—I mean gal."

"Ayuh," agreed Tommy.

"Well.." muttered Ma when she saw that there was a puppy in the bundle Louie carried.

"Now, Ma'm…" Cap'n Bowline started.

"Guess you're all here to help me make up my mind about this dog business."

"Here Ma—just look how cute she is," Louie put the bundle in Ma's arms.

The puppy licked the back of her hand and wiggled out of her blanket and made a little puddle on the parlor floor.

"See," Ma said, "now just who's going to break her of pissing in the house?"

Louie got a rag and cleaned up the puddle. Then he and Tommy took the puppy into the kitchen while the others settled down in the parlor. They fenced in a place in the corner of the kitchen and put a blanket down for the puppy to sleep on. She was now yawning in Louie's arms.

"This will be my last worshipping time here on the island," Uncle Sam announced, "my summer visit'n is over and my church needs me full-time now."

They sang some hymns and then Uncle Sam told a story about Jesus falling asleep in the back of the boat after a busy day of preaching and healing.

"A storm came up suddenly—as storms do on a lake. The waves were huge and the boat tossed and turned. But Jesus slept on. The storm didn't seem to bother him even though everyone else in the boat was scared to death. Someone finally shook Jesus awake. 'Can't you do something?' They demanded, 'Don't you see the boat is going to sink and we're all going to drown?' Jesus rubbed the sleep out of his eyes and looked at the frightened men around him. He told them not to be afraid. Then he held out his hands and the wind died down."

They held hands and said the Lord's Prayer together.

After worship, Mrs. Bowline helped Ma fix a feast with corn on the cob and tomatoes from the Bowlines' garden. While they ate, they talked about storms they'd all experienced.

Captain Bowline said, "Speak'n of storms, he'rd there was a hurricane brew'n off the coast and head'n this way. Bettah batten down the hatches and git prepared. Could be a big one. Some say she'll hit land 'afore she gits here—though you never can tell about these storms. They're sure fickle—like womenfolk."

"There's another storm—only it's an inland one," said Uncle Sam, "and it's about sports—all about who has the best baseball team."

Now Louie was all ears.

"Some call it the survival of the fittest."

Louie worried about storms at sea—sometimes those involved survival, too. But he turned back to the inland storm; it was safer to think about. He'd heard about the battle between the National League baseball teams and the American League teams—which League was the best. He knew who his best team was—the Boston Pilgrims, now called the Americans because they had beaten all the other teams in the American League.

"The leagues are finally going to play each other this fall, " continued Uncle Sam, "It will be the first world championship games. Hope our Boston team wins them all."

"We'll say *Amen* to that!" agreed Louie and Tommy in unison.

Their cheer woke up the puppy. They heard her whimper and whine from her new corner nest.

Mrs. Bowline said to Ma.

"She's in a strange place and away from her ma, brothers, and sisters. It will be lonely for her for a while."

Louie went over to the puppy and picked her up. She nuzzled under his arm and stopped whimpering. Would Ma finally consent to let him keep this precious puppy he so badly wanted?

Ma spoke to both Mrs. Bowline and the Captain.

"Guess that means you brought her—not expecting to take her back with you."

Captain Bowline looked sheepish and said, "Sally's weaned them so we got to find new homes for 'em. We thought ye needed a sea dog on this here island."

Louie prayed and crossed his fingers. He was about to burst, waiting for Ma's response.

Ma sighed as she watched Louie hugging the puppy.

"All right—you all win. Louie does need a new pet."

September 14, 1903. Winds E 10-15. Cool. Clear.
New dog arrives. Other visitors: Captain Bowline,
Mrs. Bowline, Tommy, and Sam Hornblower.

—Louie Hollander

CHAPTER 7

Miracles

Louie lost sleep taking care of the new puppy.

When he put the puppy down for the night, she cried and cried. So Louie lay down beside her until it was his turn to man the light beacon. Then he carried her under his arms when he went up the lighthouse stairs to fill the reservoir and trim the wick. Finally, he took the puppy to bed with him. She burrowed under the covers and lay down at his feet.

"What will you name her?" Ma asked the next morning. Louie thought and thought about it all day. Maybe he'd call her Burrows because she loved to snuggle under his arm or under the quilt on his bed. Maybe he'd call her Dusty because her coat wasn't pure white.

He tried these names out but none seemed to fit her as a sea dog. Sea dogs—just what did they do? Louie thought about that while he milked Betsy and gathered eggs.

Betsy mooed loudly and swished her tail when the puppy came near.

"Now Betsy, " soothed Louie, "she's not going to bother you."

But when Louie started to milk the cow, the puppy jumped up to try to get some of the milk before it went into the pail. That did it. Betsy kicked up her hoofs and knocked over the milk pail. Louie found himself covered with milk and sprawled on the ground with his puppy licking milk off his face.

"It was a miracle you both weren't hurt," Ma said.

The chickens put on a screeching fit when they spied the puppy. Feathers and fur flew. Louie had to finally put the puppy down in her kitchen box so he could concentrate on gathering eggs.

"They'll get used to you," he told the puppy as he rubbed her tummy to soothe her fright. "They'll have to because you're going to be a lighthouse keeper, too."

That afternoon he went through the package that Captain Bowline had brought him from Miss Gilbert. The package contained another Mark Twain book as she had promised, *The Prince and the Pauper,* as well as a geometry book. On top of a sheaf of papers, lay a letter from Miss Gilbert.

Dear Louie,

I hope you enjoy reading this book by Mark Twain that he wrote before he wrote *Tom Sawyer* and *Huckleberry Finn.* I've also enclosed an article in the *Sacramento Daily Union* that Mark Twain penned while he was in Hawaii in 1866. He wrote the article after interviewing and reading the journals of Captain Josiah Mitchell and Samuel and Henry Ferguson. These men made a 4,000 mile voyage in 43 days in a longboat with only a ten day provision of food and water after their clipper ship, *the Hornet,* burned at sea. It has been reported that this article made Samuel Clemens—that's Mark Twain's real name—famous as a writer. After you have finished reading it, write a paper about the miracle of their reaching Hawaii alive and why you think they survived. Answer the question, "What light guided them?" Make a map tracing their journey. Then do the exercises in the first five chapters of the geometry book.

See you when I next make rounds.

—Miss Gilbert

Louie put the papers and books aside to go up to the lighthouse tower to get the beacon ready for the night. He held up the puppy to the glass tower windows so she could see out to sea.

"See those ships," he told her pointing to some steamers passing by. "You're going to help me scout them."

"How do you like that, Scout?" Louie patted her head. The puppy woofed—contented. "Scouts are really boys and girls but I think dogs should be scouts, too. You're going to be a sea scout."

Just then a seagull landed on the railing.

Louie had seen lots of seagulls at night landing near the lighted lamp but this one looked vaguely familiar.

"Sammy? Could that be you?"

The seagull cawed and flapped both his wings.

Louie held the puppy up to the glass window to meet Sammy.

"Sammy—meet Scout."

But Sammy turned his back and flew off into the night.

"Don't leave," Louie called as he watched his old pet disappear. Then he turned and took his new pet down the tower steps.

CHAPTER 8

Storm Clouds

September 15, 1903. Barometer falling. Wind gusts from SE up to 40 knots. Prepared for hurricane.

—Louie Hollander

They heard the wind first.

Ma shook him awake. It was still dark outside.

"Wha-a-a-t's wrong?" Louie rubbed the sleep from his eyes and sat up. Scout peeked his head out from the comfort of the quilt.

"We've not much time before the hurricane gets here. Got to batten down the hatches," Ma said.

Louie dressed quickly. Although he'd been in bad storms before, they'd had Pa with them to help weather them. Now it was just the two of them. His stomach churned.

But Ma was all business.

"Let's get those shutters closed, then we'll check the beacon," she said.

Louie latched the dormer windows first. Then he followed Ma down the loft steps and they both worked together to latch the wooden shutters on the first floor.

Louie put Scout in her corner bed. She whimpered so he gave her some milk. Then he found some plywood in the chicken shed. With the kerosene lantern in one hand, he took the plywood in the other up the winding lighthouse tower steps just in case. He checked the wick. It was still burning.

By this time the first light of dawn was breaking through the gathering clouds so he could see out over the ocean. Whitecaps rushed toward shore. The oncoming waves dashed against the rocks.

"Make sure there's enough coal for the fog siren machine," Ma called from the bottom of the steps.

Louie took the bucket and went down the steep steps to the coal shed and filled it. He made several trips just to make sure—bending over and holding the bucket tight against his chest when a gust of wind hit him.

"What about Betsy?" Louie asked Ma.

"Go milk her, give her some hay, and then latch the shed door."

With Scout at his heels, Louie finished the milking just in time. By now an angry sea was spending her fury with surges of water that splashed against the rocks sending up large bursts of white spray. Each wave that made it up onto the shoreline bounded back to meet the next wave, making more white water. Meanwhile, dark gray clouds racing across the sky began to release sheets of rain.

Louie latched the door to the cowshed, picked up Scout in one arm, and started carrying the milk sloshing in the pail back to the house. Scout wiggled out of Louie's arm and ran back to the cowshed sniffing the air.

"Scout, come here!" Louie called above the howling wind. He put the pail down and caught Scout just as she was climbing a dangerous rock. He hadn't had time to teach her to come when he called her name.

"Good girl," he patted her head. "This is not time to go for a swim. You're not old enough yet."

Louie put his arm around Scout. Before he picked up the milk bucket, he turned to see if anything else needed securing.

CHAPTER 9

Hurricane

The rowboat was not safe!

Even though she was on high ground now, the tide was coming in and the wave surge would soon reach her. *Must get her to higher ground*, thought Louie. But what would he do with Scout? He didn't want to let her go again. He'd try to drag the boat with one hand to higher ground.

He reached the boat, untied the painter, and began to pull. But he was too late. A wave slithered in and sent its spray over the boat and Louie's head. Louie slipped on the wet rocks and lost both the boat and Scout, who jumped and followed the receding wave back down to the angry sea.

"No, Scout! No! Come back!" screamed Louie over the wind's roar.

Then Louie saw the oar, just beyond Scout. It had fallen out of the boat and the receding wave was carrying it back out to sea. Louie sloshed through the water and grabbed the oar with one hand and Scout by the scruff of her neck with the other. He crawled back up the rocks on his back clutching both the oar and Scout until he reached higher ground.

He found a piece of line in the boat shed and tied it around Scout's neck and then to the boat post. With Scout now secure from following the next crashing wave, Louie pulled the double-ender rowboat up as far as he could away from the roaring sea.

Then he tied a stern line to the post and the boat's painter to a higher rock.

The rain began to come crosswise in sheets as he carried Scout and the milk pail back to the house. He handed his wet clothes and the watery milk to Ma. She hung his wet clothes by the coal stove and put the milk into a jug.

Louie told Ma all about how the puppy had seen the oar being carried out to sea before he had.

"She lived up to a Newfoundland's reputation. She ran to retrieve the lost oar."

It was getting darker now. The wind screamed and the shutters clattered.

"Hope they hold," Ma said. "Let's get that fog siren started."

Louie and Ma put on their oilskins, made sure the door was latched, and went back out into the storm. They clung to each other and kept their heads down so they wouldn't lose their footing on the slippery rocks. The trip seemed to take forever. Finally they made it out to the fog siren shed and cranked up the engine until it coughed and started.

"Now the light beacon. Got to trim the wicks."

Again, they made their dangerous way back up the hill to the lighthouse tower. When they reached the Fresnel lamp, the tower seemed to sway with every wind gust. Louie wound the clockwork while Ma filled the reservoir. She was trimming the wick when they heard a loud noise.

"Ma watch out!"

At first, Louie thought Ma had fallen down the stairs, just as Pa had during the storm at Swanton Point. Then he realized Ma had jumped aside and hit the brass dustpan.

She had gotten out of the way just before the glass pane splintered onto the floor. Rain began to pour in. The wind followed and blew out the lamp wick. Suddenly it was dark. Louie reached around to grab something and his hand brushed against Ma. Then he heard her voice.

"Quick Louie grab that plywood behind you."

Louie groped around the tower wall behind him for the piece of plywood he had brought up earlier. He picked it up and placed it over the broken glass pane. Together he and Ma pushed it over the opening. It took all the strength he had just to hold it in place while the wind tried to push it back into the tower.

"You'll have to hold it there until I get the hammer and some nails."

Ma left him and went down the tower steps.

"Careful, Ma." Louie did not want her falling down those winding stairs, as Pa had done. He couldn't bear to lose both of them.

Louie braced his feet as best he could against the base of the Fresnel lens turning mechanism and pushed hard against the back of the plywood. Each time a gust of wind pushed on the other side Louie willed his arms to stay straight and not buckle. It seemed like an eternity until Ma was back at his side with the hammer and nails—none too soon because Louie's strength was ebbing fast.

Ma relit the kerosene lantern first, then the lamp wick on the fuel jet. She helped Louie nail the plywood over the broken window. Louie found a broom and cleaned up the broken glass.

"I'll stay in the tower for a while, just in case another glass pane should break," Louie offered.

Ma said she would spell him after she checked out the fog siren.

Between the sounds of the furious waves dashing against the rocks and the wind howling, Louie heard another familiar sound.

"Kuk! Kuk!"

Following the light from the lamp he caught a glimpse of a seagull perched on the railing.

"Sammy!" Louie cried. "I'm so glad you found your way through the hurricane."

Sammy cocked his head to one side. Louie noted that when Sammy tried to flap his wings they wouldn't move. His feathers were too matted and the wind was too strong. Louie waited for a lull in the winds then opened the tower door a crack so the drenched bird could fly in.

CHAPTER 10

Clean Up

September 17, 1903. Weathered hurricane #2 with minimal damage. Wind gusts up to 85. Kept light burning and fog-horn sounding.

—Louie Hollander

We did it Ma!

We kept the light burning and fog siren going."

Louie heaved a sigh of relief as he took off his dripping oilskin and plunked down in the nearest chair. With the sun up and the hurricane past, Ma had just returned from extinguishing the wick on the light beacon.

"Remember, we did have to relight the lamp wick once," she reminded him.

Louie could barely keep his eyes open. He couldn't hold back the yawns. After his turn in the tower with Sammy by his side, he had added coal to the fog siren engine. He'd maneuvered his way carefully over wet rocks with his back to the wind and his head down through the passageway into the house to find a whimpering puppy. No sooner had he quieted her down when he heard Betsy mooing outside and had to let her in, too.

"Now it's time to get these animals outside, since the wind and rain have stopped, and assess the damage," Ma said.

All Louie wanted to do was to lie down on his bed in the loft. Instead, he had to take Betsy back down to the shed. It no longer had a roof and the door was ajar on its hinges. Louie tied the cow to the post that still held the double ender. Scout followed at his heels. All around lay the flotsam brought in by the storm—seaweed, bottles, broken pieces of wood, and masses of rope. Louie found the roof in two pieces among the mess and dragged it back to the shed.

He climbed up and over the hill to other side of the island to see how the pier and wharf had survived the storm. He could see from the top of the hill that the wharf was still standing. But when he inspected more closely, he discovered that several of the top boards had been washed out to sea. He looked over at the coal shed and sighed. *Bet the coal has gotten real wet during the storm,* he thought.

By now Louie was blinking his eyes to stay awake. He dragged himself back up to the house. Ma had a breakfast of eggs and bread waiting for him. But Louie fell asleep at the table.

During the next three days Louie and Ma repaired all the damage created by the hurricane. Louie had just begun to pile all the new pieces of driftwood the storm had washed up on shore behind the cow shed when he heard an unfamiliar boat whistle coming from the direction of the wharf. He dropped the wood, then ran up and over the hill to the other side of the island. A sloop propelled by an inboard engine had pulled up alongside the wharf.

"Brought yer mail," shouted the man at the helm.

"New mail boat, too?" returned Louie.

He came down the steep steps with a barking Scout at his heels and caught the lines tossed by the mailman, cleating them tightly.

The mailman handed over a packet of envelopes.

"Name's Gus."

"Thanks, Gus. When will you be back?"

"'Speck about two days, weather permittin','" Gus shouted over the din of the motor as Louie tossed the lines back into the sloop. The mailman gunned up her engine and sped off for the next island delivery.

Louie peeled off the string wrapped around the packet and leafed through the envelopes without waiting for Ma who had started down the steps to meet him. He took out two letters addressed to him to read and handed the rest to Ma.

Hey Louie!

How'd ye fare in that storm? Did the lamp go out? Ma and most of the women folk are pacing their widow's walks keeping vigil and hoping to see their men folk's fishing schooners come home. None have returned yet and we're prayin' they all arrive back safely. They're worried that some of them may not have survived the hurricane. Even though the eye went to the south of us, the waves were huge! I watched the waves as they hit the shore in front of our house. They knocked down one of the fishing piers and we've all been put to work trying to rebuild it 'afore the fishing fleet returns.

Here's cross hand'n ye.

—Charlie

Louie folded the letter and slid it back in the envelope. He opened the second letter and read it when he got back to the house.

CHAPTER 11

The Invitation

"**M**a, can I go?"

Louie leapt up from his chair and showed the letter to Ma.

"Go where?" Ma looked up from opening and reading her letters.

"To the Game…in Boston…with Uncle Sam!"

"What are you babbling about, Louie? Here sit back down and let me read that letter."

Dear Louie,

I'm back at my church but miss my visits with you and your mother. We've just formed a new youth group here—boys all about your age—Matthew, Dan, Billy, and Caleb. We met for the first time to plan our activities for the fall. On everyone's wish list was going to a baseball game, preferably one of the world championship games in Boston. Well, I wrote to Henry Killilea, the owner of the American League Ball Club, who attended worship one Sunday this summer, and he sent me eight tickets to the opening games on October 1st and 2nd. Of course

I want you and Charlie to go with us. You can take the steamer from there and meet us at the train station on the 30th. Plan to be gone for about five days. We'll camp out at the Huntington Fair grounds for two nights and spend one day and one night on the train. You may need to spend Saturday night with me in order to get the steamer back to town on Sunday. Hope your Ma will give her permission. Write me back.

—Uncle Sam

"Well, can I?" Louie leaned over toward Ma and waited expectantly.

Ma put down the letter to open the rest of her mail. She sighed.

"I wish I could let you go—but I can't…"

Louie's face fell and his fist pounded the table.

"Louie…" Ma looked him in the eye and touched his arm. "I need you here to tend the lamp, take care of the animals, and work on your lessons. We missed almost a week of your schooling repairing the damage from the hurricane."

She shook her head, no.

"But Ma…" Louie argued, "I haven't been away from this old island except for a few hours when I went to Captain Bowline's house."

"No." Ma repeated.

"I never get to do anything. I can't have friends over. I can't play baseball. I can't wear clothes like the other boys wear. At least let me go this once to see a world championship baseball game!"

The more Louie cajoled and argued the only answer he got was a firm, no.

"You don't care about me!" Louie screamed at his mother, "All you care about is that stupid lamp!" Louie stomped up the steps to his loft room. Scout woofed and followed at his heels.

"When you calm down, come downstairs and write back to both Charlie and Uncle Sam. You'll have to tell them both that your old ogre of a mother can't let you go with them to the games. Sorry, Louie, but that's how it has to be."

CHAPTER 12

Lessons

Louie wouldn't speak to Ma.

When Louie handed Gus the two letters he had dutifully written, he wouldn't speak to him either. He was still mad. Besides not letting him go with Uncle Sam, Charlie, and the other boys to the games, she had made him sit down and work on his lessons.

Louie finished his geometry lessons. But when it came to writing the paper Miss Gilbert had assigned to him about the longboat and its survivors, he didn't have the heart for it. He drew the map first, then wrote a few short sentences:

"Freedom was the light that guided the men in that boat; freedom from women and freedom from school work. They were just plain lucky to get to go to Hawaii."

Ma finally told him to go. "Go anywhere. Just get some of that piss and vinegar out of your system."

Louie stormed out the door, slamming it behind him almost catching Scout's tail. He headed for his favorite spot to sit and read under the two trees. But he didn't feel like reading and he didn't feel like writing. He looked over at the double-ender boat nearby.

He could take that boat and row away from Ma and this island and never come back. He picked up some small stones and started throwing them into the ocean. If he threw bigger ones they'd make a bigger splash. Just as he was trying to loosen a huge rock to throw, he heard a shout.

"Stop. We're friends not foe!"

Louie looked up and saw a dory approaching with Mr. McAllister seated in the stern and Miss Gilbert perched on the bow seat.

Great, he thought. *Just what I need—those two.*

Louie scowled as he hooked the dory to the chain and hauled up the boat. The seamen got out and helped Miss Gilbert out of the dory with her satchel of books carried on a rope in one hand.

Miss Gilbert looked at Louie and said,

"Louie, you look like the Old Lady who swallowed the fly. You OK?"

Louie grunted, "Sure," and followed her and Mr. McAllister up to the house.

As Miss Gilbert hung up her bonnet on the peg, Ma said, "Don't mind Louie. He's just mad at me because I couldn't let him go to the world championship games in Boston with Sam Hornblower. I couldn't let him go because I need him to help man the lamp."

She turned to Louie.

"Go with Miss Gilbert while I talk to Mr. McAllister in the kitchen."

Louie hated both of them, too, but he followed Miss Gilbert into the parlor.

"Here," she said opening her satchel, "I brought you another Mark Twain book, his newest, *A Connecticut Yankee in King Arthur's Court,* and I finally found a good reader, *Lights to Literature.* Thought you'd like this better than that juvenile McGuffey's reader."

Louie took the two books from Miss Gilbert, looked at the covers, and then put them down again.

"Now show me your map and what you wrote about how that longboat reached Hawaii without food and water. Next I'll check your geometry lessons."

Louie handed Miss Gilbert the map he had made of the Hornet's journey in the Pacific Ocean and the subsequent wanderings of the longboats carrying the survivors after the disastrous fire.

"You've done this well. Now how about the essay I asked you to write."

Louie handed her the paper he had written and mumbled under this breath, "I'm not sure this is what you wanted."

Miss Gilbert scowled.

"You can do better than this. Please look over the story and rewrite this."

She handed the paper back to Louie.

Louie shrugged his shoulders.

Miss Gilbert gave him some new assignments and then got up to leave.

Louie ushered Miss Gilbert and Mr. McAllister to the waiting dory, then sauntered back up to the house. He took the new books up to the loft and stayed there until time to light the lamp wick.

When he returned from the lighthouse tower, Ma had a supper of fish chowder ready for him on the kitchen table. She hummed and smiled at Louie as she spooned the chowder into his bowl. Louie kept his head down and started slurping the soup to drown out the tune she was humming. It sounded to him like she was humming, "Take me out to the ball game…" and he didn't want to hear that song so he slurped louder.

At last she stopped humming and spoke.

"Mr. McAllister told me that he'd send Aussie to help me tend the lamp and help with lighthouse chores so you'd be able to go with the youth group to…."

Louie's spoon clattered on the table and he jumped up, nearly knocking over the soup bowl. He gave Ma a great big hug before she could finish her sentence.

Ma laughed. She hugged him back.

"I'm glad you can go, Louie. Mr. McAllister said he'd send Uncle Sam a telegram tonight. Now go up and find your duffel. They'll pick you up in a few days."

"And I'm sorry I was such a jerk. Thanks, Ma," Louie called as he leapt up the steps to the loft two by two and grabbed his duffel.

September 27, 1903: Wind SE 15. Mr. McAllister brings Miss Gilbert. He's sending Aussie to relieve me so I can go to the World Series!

—Louie Hollander

CHAPTER 13

Steaming South

Louie tossed his duffel and bedroll into the bow.
He nearly collided with Aussie as Aussie stepped out of the dory with his own duffel.

Scout jumped into the waiting dory next.

"No, Scout, you can't go." Louie's only regret on going was leaving his new puppy behind.

"Take good care of her, Ma!" Scout wiggled in Ma's arms and tried to get free.

"Off you go, Louie. Here I almost forgot, buy yourself a baseball cap and some souvenirs with this." She thrust a two-dollar bill into his hands. Yesterday, she had given him money for the steamer and train fares. She even made a lunch in a basket for him to take on the steamer ride.

"Mr. McAllister ask'd if I'd give ye this…"

Aussie handed him a dollar bill.

Wow, Louie thought. *I'm rich*. He was so excited he almost lost his balance.

"Don't rock the boat!" A sailor shouted. Louie pocketed the money and waved goodbye.

The boat trip into town seemed to Louie to last forever. He was anxious about not missing the steamer when she stopped. But the dory arrived an hour before steamer docking time. Louie sat on the town dock and busied himself counting the lobster traps and reading one of the *Boy's Life* magazines he'd brought along.

Louie heard the bell and saw the smoke before he could distinguish the *Dewline*, the excursion steamer.

Then, as she approached the town wharf, he observed passengers moving around her open decks.

The *Dewline* tied up alongside the wharf and put up her gangway. Louie stood aside when the seaman opened the rope gate to let off passengers. A couple—a portly man guiding a full-figured woman—got off first. One of the man's diamond studs popped off his waistcoat and landed at Louie's feet as the man huffed and puffed up the gangway. When Louie stooped to retrieve the diamond before it rolled into the water, the lady's bandbox hit him in the head.

Louie handed the man the precious button while rubbing his forehead.

"Sir. I think you lost something."

The man pocketed the diamond and handed Louie a half dollar.

"Here you are, son."

Once again Louie almost said "I'm not your son" but when the steward called, "Anyone coming aboard? Next land'n is Bath," he forgot the insult and replied, "I am, sir."

With lunch basket in one hand, bed roll under one arm, and duffel over his shoulder, Louie walked down the gangway onto the deck. He tried to find a place to sit on the bow. Many of the other passengers on the ship wanted to stand or sit in the bow space, too. Some hung over the front rail and others sat on folding campstools. Louie sat on his bedroll and watched the crew as they released the lines and pushed the boat away from the wharf.

The *Dewline* puffed and belched black smoke as she backed around and headed out of Windlass Bay. With each turn of the steam piston Louie could feel the excitement in every bone and joint in his body.

The bow space emptied as the sea grew rougher out on the open ocean. All the passengers on deck went inside except Louie. Louie marveled as the captain of the *Dewline* maneuvered his ship up and around the swells while the boilers chewed through coal and spit out steam to drive the pistons. Louie lasted as long as he could until he felt chilled and damp from the ocean water spraying onto the bow. He picked up his duffel and found an empty seat as far away from the cigar smokers as he could inside the cabin. A red-faced whiskered man and a girl with blond curls holding a basket on her lap sat beside him. The girl turned and smiled at him.

She's about my age, he thought, *and so pretty, too.* He felt awkward beside her.

The red-faced whiskered man turned to Louie and said, "Where you headed?"

"I'm going to the world championship games in Boston."

All heads around turned to look at Louie. Someone whistled.

"Wow, you're one lucky lad," another man chimed in.

The girl beside him just grinned more. She took a biscuit out of her basket and offered it to Louie.

"Want one?" She asked, "My mom made lots. My name's Louisa Ann. What's yours?

"Louie." He blushed. He took the biscuit and offered her half his fish sandwich. Some folks sitting around them were not eating. Instead their faces had turned green and they looked sick. A few got up and leaned their heads over the railing around the decks and fed the fish.

"That's my dad, Mr. Peabody," Louisa Ann said.

"How-de-do," the red-faced whiskered man said. He leaned over and shook Louie's hand vigorously.

Louisa Ann continued, "He's taking me back to my boarding school in Boston. Maybe you can come and see me after the games and tell me all about them." Her blonde curls swished when she talked.

Louie took a long time answering. Finally he blurted out, "Maybe." He almost added, *But I'll be with other guys and you might like them better than me.*

Louisa Ann wrote down the address of her school.

"Where do you go to school?" she asked Louie.

"On an island," he told her. Then he told her about Miss Gilbert bringing school books and lessons to island children who couldn't make it to the mainland for school. He also told her about light-house keepers and acknowledged that he helped his mother tend Two Tree Island Light.

When the *Dewline* reached Bath late in the day, Louie had in-vited her to come and visit him next summer. When it was time to disembark and the steward offered to help them with their belong-ings, Louie refused. Instead he carried his own duffel and bedroll, as well as his lunch basket and Louisa Ann's.

He put them all down and waved at two familiar figures. Charlie reached Louie first with the usual greeting, "How y'doin'?" Uncle Sam gave him a great bear hug. Louie stammered and remembered to introduce Louisa Ann who stood beside him.

"Meet Louisa Ann Peabody. She's going back to school in Boston."

Now four other boys gathered round. Uncle Sam introduced first Caleb, who had red hair and freckles; then Matthew, who had brown hair and bangs down over his eyes. Instead of shaking hands, Matthew just grinned at Louisa Ann. Billy, shorter than all the other boys, and his brother, Dan, finally introduced themselves to Louie and Louisa Ann. Then Uncle Sam introduced Mr. Peabody to Charlie and the other boys. He explained to Mr. Peabody that they needed to be on their way.

"The train leaves about three hours from now from Stowaway. We still have a buggy ride ahead of us."

"We're taking that train, too. Would some of you like to ride with us in our horseless carriage?" Louisa Ann's father pointed to a red automobile parked nearby. All the boys crowded round the shiny new contraption.

They oohed and awed, then said almost in unison.

"Can I ride in it?"

"Sorry, I can only take two of you young men."

After much discussion as to how they would choose who would ride in the automobile, Uncle Sam took off his cap and wrote names on slips of paper, folded each, and put all the pieces in the cap.

"Now Louisa Ann, would you do me the honor?"

One by one Louisa Ann drew out two names, Billy and Charlie.

Louie felt cheated. After all, he had met Louisa Ann first and he certainly didn't want anyone else horning in. Louie hoped that the automobile would make so much noise they wouldn't be able to talk to Louisa Ann sitting beside her father in the front seat. He joined the others reluctantly in the horse drawn buggies.

The vehicles set off together. The horse drawn buggies beat the red horseless automobile to the train station. The automobile could only go ten miles per hour and kept stalling.

Charlie told them later. "Billy and I had to get out and wind her up twice before the engine would turn over."

Two trains waited on the tracks. The local Stowaway train had the smaller engine. The other train had more cars and a big John Bull[12] engine. Louie stood beside the cowcatcher[13] on the front of the train and admired the big wheels. He felt like a dwarf beside a big giant. He had been on other trains but had never seen one with an engine so large. *Must take a lot of coal to bail into that steam engine,* he thought, as he gazed at the long firebox. *Glad I don't have the job as the fireman on this train!*

A porter carried Louisa Ann and her father's valises and helped them board the sleeping car. Uncle Sam had tickets in one of the windowed carriages with ten seats.

"We're roughing it boys," he told them as they watched Louisa Ann disappear into the sleeper car.

Two other people were already seated in their carriage car. They took one look at the six boys descending on them and asked the conductor to transfer them to another car.

"Great," Matthew said, "then we can have the whole car to ourselves."

Louie put his stuff into the overhead netting. The other boys just dumped theirs wherever there was a space.

"We've got some time before the train is due to leave, so let's get some food. Come on, Louie," Uncle Sam called. Louie wasn't sure whether the butterflies in his stomach were hunger pangs or just excitement. He helped carry the *Moxies*, corn dogs, and snacks Mr. Burke, Billy and Dan's dad, had bought from the eatery[14] onto the train.

"All aboard!" the conductor called as they hurried back to their seats.

Chug-a-chug-a. They were off to Boston. Louie settled himself beside Charlie as the train whistled and the wheels turned over and over carrying them to their destination.

---

[12] Built by Stevens in England, thus the name John Bull, in 1831. It is the oldest steam-powered engine.

[13] Iron pilot on front of a steam engine with extra wheels to help keep the engine on the track.

[14] Railroad snack bar.

CHAPTER 14

Crushing Crowds

Exhausted but happy.

That's the way Louie felt when they arrived at Union Station midmorning on the first day of October.

After eating supper in their seats, he and Charlie had played cards. Caleb and Matthew, who sat behind them, joined in and they all played slapjack. Soon cards were flying all around, then bed rolls, until Uncle Sam intervened.

"The conductor will kick us off the train for making such a ruckus. That means we'll miss seeing the world games."

The boys settled down. Louie talked baseball and listened to the latest school talk until they heard Uncle Sam and Mr. Burke snoring.

Matthew said, "Let's see if we can find where Louisa Ann is sleeping and wake her up."

The six boys tiptoed to the end of the car and made a mad dash for the next. They inspected every carriage car until they reached the sleeper car. They had knocked on three compartment doors asking for Louisa Ann when a tousled head appeared out of one of the doors.

"Get out of here. You're disturbing our sleep. If you don't leave right away I'll call the conductor to kick you off this train."

Suddenly the train lurched to a stop and the boys walked backward as fast as they could through the stopped cars. They darted into washrooms when they saw the conductor coming. But they were back in their own car before he could catch up to them.

"Let's pretend to be asleep," Louie whispered to the others when the conductor came through their car. When he left, they all did sleep; Louie, with his feet draped over Charlie; Caleb and Dan, on their bedrolls in the aisle. The others fell sleep, limbs and arms entwined with each other. At times during the night the carriage car got so hot Louie had to open the window. When he did, soot from the engine came in, so he closed it again. A sooty taste was in his mouth when the train finally pulled into Union Station.

Uncle Sam and Mr. Burke led the boys off the train into one of the waiting streetcars. Louie looked back and saw Louisa Ann being ushered by her father into a waiting buggy and waved. He nudged Charlie, "There she is!" Charlie was too busy squeezing into the streetcar to notice.

When they got off at the stop for the campgrounds, Uncle Sam and Mr. Burke found a place where they could store their bedrolls and duffels. Louie noted the factories nearby and hoped that they didn't give off any more soot. He'd had enough of that from the train.

"We can walk from here," Uncle Sam said, "just don't stray far from the two of us. We must stay together."

Louie felt the crush of the crowds even before he reached the ticket gate. He didn't like being surrounded by so many people and wished for moment he was back on Two Tree Island.

When they finally reached the gate, Uncle Sam handed over their tickets and the usher pointed them to the bleachers. Louie looked and didn't see a single seat left! People were even standing behind the bleachers.

"Guess they sold more tickets than they had seats for sitting," Dan said.

"What'll we do?"

"Just have to stand or sit on that outfield fence over there," Charlie said.

"Good watching from that fence."

"Hold on so you don't fall," Mr. Burke called as Louie and the other boys climbed to the top of the fence. They found some empty places to sit and watch the game while Mr. Burke and Uncle Sam leaned against the fence below them.

From his spot on top of the fence Louie could see the Boston team came out onto the field and heard the names of the players over the loud speaker.

Manager Jimmy Collins!
Chuck Stahl, center fielder!
Buck Freeman, right fielder!
Bill Dinneen, pitcher!
Candy LaChance, first baseman!
Hobe Ferris, second baseman!
Patsy Dougherty, left fielder!
Fred Parent, shortstop!
Lou Criger, catcher!
Cy Young, pitcher!

The word "Boston" was spelled out in red across each player's white jersey. Each was dressed in blue socks and each had on a white cap with a blue band around the base.

Have to get one of those caps as a souvenir, Louie thought.

When Cy Young took the field everyone stood, cheered, and tossed their caps into the air. They even cheered when the Pittsburgh Pirates, led by Honus Wagner, took the field.

In spite of the fact the rival leagues had been creating quite a storm for two years, both teams were recognized as good ball players. Today they would begin to battle out who was the best. Nothing else in the world mattered this day except this contest.

When the bell in the South Church Tower struck three, Young strode to the mound and the game was on. Only two minutes into the game at the end of the first inning and the Pirates were ahead 4-0. By the end of the fourth inning, Louie and Charlie were yelling with the others to take out Young as pitcher. Then came the eventful seventh inning and Freeman scored Boston's first run of the game! The crowd went wild.

Louie, Charlie, Dan, Billy, Caleb, and Matthew joined the cheering from their places on top of the fence. Charlie waved both hands in the air, lost his balance, and fell outside the fence.

Uncle Sam pushed through the crowd at the gate to get to Charlie while Louie and the others turned to look down at Charlie. A crowd gathered around him.

Louie called to Charlie, "Are you hurt?"

"Stay still!" a man in a hat said, "'till we get some help." But Charlie tried to sit up.

"Ouch! My arm."

Louie was concerned and climbed backward down the fence to be with his friend. Uncle Sam arrived with a stretcher and some medics. They carefully carried Charlie through the crowd to a waiting wagon with a big red cross and marked "Ambulance" on the side. Uncle Sam climbed up on the wagon beside Charlie.

"I want to come, too," Louie said.

"No," Uncle Sam said firmly. "You'll miss the rest of the game."

He said to Mr. Burke, who had joined them, "If I don't get back in time I'll meet you with the other boys at the campsite."

So, while Charlie went off with Uncle Sam to get his broken arm set, Louie went back to the ball field with Mr. Burke. They all kept cheering for their Boston team. But the cheers didn't work and Boston lost to the Pittsburgh Pirates by a score of 3-7 that day.

After the game, Louie bought a Boston cap for himself and one for Charlie from one of the vendors. Mr. Burke collected a souvenir card for each boy.

"Who is this man and this place on the card?" Louie asked as they walked back to the campgrounds. He pointed to the photo of the building and the man at the top of the souvenir card.

"That's McGreevy," Mr. Burke said, "He sells the beer around here and that's his place, the Third Base Saloon." Louie remembered Charlie telling him about his pa spending all his time at the local saloon. He felt guilty because he had been able to watch until the end of the game, but Charlie hadn't.

CHAPTER 15

Play Ball

Charlie's cast made a hit.

Boys all over the campgrounds stood in line to sign it. Louie and Matthew had to take turns holding the lantern against the cast so each person in line could find writing space.

Louie's eyelids were so heavy that all he wanted to do was to unroll his bedroll with the oilskin cover and go to sleep. Even a light rain during the night didn't wake him. In the morning, by the time their group had folded up their bedrolls, washed up, and eaten breakfast at a nearby eatery, the rain had picked up.

Uncle Sam conferred with Mr. Burke and then announced, "There's a traveling circus in a tent on the grounds where we'll spend our morning. Afterward, we'll head over to the ballpark early so we can get seats for this game. I don't want you boys fence-sitting and falling again. One broken arm is enough!"

By noon the rain had slowed to a light drizzle and they had all found seats in the bleachers. When he played on the Swanton Point team, Louie had often tried to imitate Bill Dinneen's pitching. He savored each moment watching him throw his hypnotic curve balls during this important game. When the American Pilgrims came up to bat, Patsy Dougherty drove in the first run. Louie jumped up and down with the other boys when Hobe Ferris made his fantastic catch in the fourth inning. Then, to top it off, Dougherty made a home run in the sixth inning. All the crowd stood up as one body and said, "Ah!" and "Oh!"

"We won!" Louie slapped hands with Charlie and then with the other boys.

"2 to 0!"

As the game ended crowds of people descended onto the ball field. Louie leapt down from the bleachers with Dan, Matthew, and Charlie following. *I must get Dougherty's autograph* was his only thought.

"Stop!" called Uncle Sam. But Louie and the others kept running.

The four boys joined the crowd surrounding the team carrying Dougherty on their shoulders. Once again Louie had that uncomfortable feeling of being swallowed by a throbbing mass of people.

"Lift me up!" he shouted.

Dan and Matthew hoisted him up so he could sit between them with one leg on each of their shoulders. In this position he was on a level with Dougherty. The three boys then pushed their way through the crowd until they could get close to Dougherty. Louie leaned over as far as he could without falling and thrust his ball into Dougherty's hands. Dougherty signed it with a flourish of his pen and handed it back as someone else in the crowd thrust another ball at him.

A big black wagon with "Third Base Saloon" written in red on the side drove right onto the ball field passing out free beer to anyone who would take a bottle. Charlie, who was behind the other two boys, grabbed a bottle with his free arm and took a swig.

"Great stuff," he said to Louie over the din of the crowd, "here have swig."

Louie shook his head. He just kept walking as if in a daze, not believing he now possessed an autographed baseball.

Matthew, now walking between Charlie and Louie, started to take the bottle from Charlie.

"I will."

"Aw, get your own. This is mine." Charlie finished the bottle and threw it onto the ground. Louie grabbed Matthew's arm and steered him away from the beer distributing truck and back to join the others.

"Okay, let's count heads," Mr. Burke said when Louie, Dan, and Matthew got back to the bleachers.

"Charlie seems to be the only one missing now except for Uncle Sam who went looking for you boys. We won't move from here until both of them return."

While Mr. Burke counted heads, Louie showed the others his autographed ball. He just couldn't believe that he had Dougherty's autograph. Then Uncle Sam returned guiding Charlie by his good arm.

"Ok, boys. I'm glad none of you got trampled."

Uncle Sam looked right at Louie. "Didn't you hear me calling you to stop?"

"No Sir."

"Taking off like that was not a good idea, Louie. I would hate to bring any more of you home battered and bruised.

And Charlie—you look a little green around the gills. Your arm bothering you?"

"Nope," Charlie answered.

CHAPTER 16

Dilemma

D on't you dare tell!"

Charlie whispered in Louie's ear on their way back to the campgrounds. All around them people were discussing the game.

"How about that double play—did you see Ferris catch Wagner's fierce liner—Dineen's pitching was first class—best ball game I've ever seen played." Even the Pirate fans agreed upon the latter. They reveled at the Pirate team's defense. Both Boston and Pittsburgh fans looked forward to the next game the following day.

"Can't we stay for the next game?' Billy pleaded over supper.

"Sorry. I'd like to stay, too, but I have to be back to preach on Sunday," Uncle Sam answered.

"Hully gee…" said all six boys in unison.

"Tomorrow we take the early morning train back to Bath. We'll need to rise with the roosters."

Louie slept fitfully that night. He worried about Charlie—about his broken arm, about his pa, and about his drinking that beer. He wondered if he should discuss his concerns with Uncle Sam, but then Charlie might get mad at him for telling.

It was five in the morning when they furled up their bedrolls, hoisted their duffels, and boarded a streetcar for Union Station. On this trip there were lots of empty seats. The train north carried half empty carriages when it pulled out of the station at six o'clock. Most of the fans who had made the trip with Louie and the youth group were staying for all the Boston championship games that weekend.

Just as the train began to pick up speed, Louie remembered Louisa Ann's invitation to visit her at her school. He wondered if he would ever see her again. Then he remembered he had her address still in his pocket. When the train makes its first stop, he'd buy a postcard and write to tell her all about the baseball games.

Uncle Sam and Mr. Burke settled down to read the *Boston Globe* extra sports edition with news of the last two games. Louie, Matthew, Billy, Caleb, and Dan played cards. Charlie sat by himself in the back of the carriage car and moaned about his arm hurting. Louie and the other boys took turns going to sit with him but Charlie wasn't interested in talking much. Before long he fell asleep.

When Louie saw that Charlie was asleep, he went to sit by Uncle Sam.

"Got something on your mind?" Uncle Sam asked.

"Yep—but don't know whether I should talk about it."

"Understand, but talking about it keeps it from festering inside."

"But if I talk about it, someone will be mad at me."

"Who's someone?"

"Charlie. I'm worried about him."

"So am I," replied Uncle Sam.

"It's his pa being lost and all. You know his pa drinks real bad. Then Charlie drank that beer.."

"What beer?" interrupted Uncle Sam.

"After the game…he took one of the free bottles being passed out… but I wasn't supposed to tell you."

"Hmm… I'm glad you did."

"And he acted as if he liked it and tried to get me and Matthew to drink it, too."

"Did you?"

"No, and I dragged Matthew away."

Louie had an uneasy feeling in the pit of his stomach. In a way he was glad that he had confided in Uncle Sam but perhaps he was being disloyal to Charlie.

CHAPTER 17

Broken Relationship

C harlie woke up when the train stopped.

All the other boys, except Charlie and Louie, got out to walk the platform with Mr. Burke. They took turns climbing up into the large engine cab with the engineer. Uncle Sam stayed with Charlie and Louie.

"Does your arm hurt?" asked Uncle Sam.

"Lots", Charlie replied.

"Did it hurt yesterday, too?" Uncle Sam continued.

"Didn't feel it much, with the excitement of the game and all," Charlie replied.

"Surprising that it didn't hurt when you disappeared into the crowd after the game with everyone pushing and shoving."

"I didn't feel anyone pushing or shoving," Charlie responded.

"Guess the beer helped with that," Uncle Sam added.

"Who told you?"

"Louie told me because he was concerned about you."

Charlie glared at Louie. "Some friend you are—see if I tell you anything anymore!"

Charlie's anger flared and Louie drew back.

"But I told Uncle Sam because I knew he cared about you, too," Louie said almost to himself. *Perhaps I should have kept the secret,* he thought.

Uncle Sam continued, "Charlie, I know how beer dulls the pain. It did that for me when I was your age. It tasted good, too, and soon I found that I depended on it to take away the edge of that pain. That can happen to you, too. I'm here if you want to talk about it with me or with Louie."

"I'm not talking to Louie. He's not my friend anymore." With that Charlie turned his back on both of them.

Louie now felt awful. Uncle Sam put his arm around him.

"You did the right thing, Louie. It will take time, but Charlie will come around."

The conductor said "All aboard" and the train started up again. Matthew, Dan, Billy, Caleb, and Mr. Burke jumped on board just as the train began to pick up steam.

"Just made it," Matthew said, "that engine is cool—I mean hot."

At the next stop, Louie joined the others at the eatery and bought two postcards, one to send to Louisa Ann and one to give to Ma. He'd bought Aussie a cap like his before leaving the ballpark to thank him for coming to help Ma man the light.

On Louisa Ann's postcard he wrote:

How's school? We got to see the first World Series game from the fence. Charlie fell off and broke his arm. I got Dougherty's autograph on my ball after Boston won the second game. Missed seeing you on the train.
Write soon.

—Louie Hollander

"Who're you writing to, Louie?" asked Billy.

When Louie told him, Billy started in, "Louie's sweet on Louisa Ann; Louisa Ann's sweet on Louie." Matthew and Dan joined in and Louie blushed.

Then, Uncle Sam started a round of singing:

"She'll be com'n round the mountain when she comes…"

Soon they were all singing—all except Charlie who still sulked in his corner of the carriage.

They sang, "Take me out to the ball game…" Then "Found a peanut…" and others until the conductor came into the carriage.

Louie thought they were going to be bawled out for making so much noise. Instead the conductor bent down and whispered something in Uncle Sam's ear. Neither man looked very happy.

The boys stopped singing and waited for the reprimand. Instead, Uncle Sam said,

"The conductor has just told me that he has received a telegram that Boston lost the third game, 2-4. Deacon Phillipe's pitching and Honus Wagner's spectacular play won the game."

The conductor spoke up.

"It was a good thing you boys weren't there. The police were called in to hold back the 20,000 people who jammed into every available space in the ball field. The players didn't even have room in the outfield to play and many spectators were hurt. Now the two teams go to Pittsburgh to continue the series. We'll have to keep telegraphing Boston to find out what happens."

But we don't have a telegraph on Two Tree Island, Louie thought. *I'll never know who wins the World Series. Why do I have to go back to that island? Why can't I live the way the rest of world lives? It's not fair.*

Louie sulked in his seat. But he didn't have long to moan because the train was slowing and Uncle Sam announced,

"Grab your gear, this is our stop."

CHAPTER 18

Lost

To Charlie's house first," Uncle Sam announced.

Louie gave the other boys a cross handshake and invited them all to come out to Two Tree Island in the summer. But Charlie ignored them all. He climbed into a carriage with Uncle Sam. Uncle Sam called to Louie, but Louie was across the road mailing his postcard to Louisa Ann.

"Shake a leg, Louie," Uncle Sam called.

Louie climbed in the carriage beside Charlie. But Charlie turned his back on Louie and wouldn't speak to him. He directed all conversation to Uncle Sam on the long buggy ride to his fishing village. He moaned constantly about his arm hurting. Louie, feeling rejected and left out, turned away and tried to sleep.

The carriage driver spent an hour trying to find Charlie's house in a cluster of houses near the shore.

"That's it, over there..." Charlie pointed while Uncle Sam held the lantern high. "That's it," echoed Louie, "I can see the widow's walk on top."

Charlie's sister burst into tears when she opened the door and saw Charlie. From the top of the stairs his mother called down.

"They didn't come back." She stifled a sob. "Sorry, come on in. We just heard the news earlier today. The rest of the fishing fleet returned but not the *Tipsy*. No one has seen her since the storm…."

Her voice trailed off, and the sobs she'd been holding back took over. When she regained her composure, she continued. "A Life Saving Service ship has been sent out from Nova Scotia to where the ships were last seen together. If she did go down, they're now searching for survivors. But the ocean is so cold near Nova Scotia…." She shivered.

"Oh Charlie!"

Suddenly she noticed that he was in the room. She came over to give him a hug and then saw his arm in a sling. "What happened? How were the games?"

Charlie gave her a kiss on her wet check.

"I'm OK, Ma—just broke my arm. The games were fun."

Uncle Sam said, "I'm sorry to hear about the *Tipsy*, but don't give up hope yet. Keep on praying for the Life Saving Service to find them all."

"I'll try," Mrs. Missen mumbled.

"Now I have Charlie here, things will be better. We all need to get some sleep. I bet you're both tired, too."

Louie yawned. He really was tired but he'd be willing to stay here with Charlie if he asked. But Charlie did not ask. Instead, it was almost as if Louie and Uncle Sam didn't exist.

"Good night, Charlie." Louie tried to give Charlie a cross handshake, but Charlie pulled away.

"I'll come back tomorrow and stay the night so I can take Charlie to the doctor's office the next day. He needs to check his arm," Uncle Sam said.

He took Louie's arm and they retreated to the waiting buggy.

In another hour Louie was dead to the outside world, comfortably asleep in the extra bed in Uncle Sam's house. He dreamt of fog and bells.

CHAPTER 19

Facing Fear

Bells were ringing.

Louie woke up with a start. What he heard weren't fog bells after all but church bells. Daylight streamed through the window. Louie didn't realize he had slept so long. He went to find Uncle Sam but he was the only one in the house. He assumed Uncle Sam had already left to be the preacher at his church. He glanced out the window again and saw people entering the front door of the white building with a towering steeple next door.

Louie checked the time on the clock in the hall. *Almost ten o'clock. Better hurry.* He wished he had brought some dress up clothes but he'd only packed clothes for the trip. He hurriedly put on his overalls. When everyone else was inside and they were singing the first hymn, Louie snuck into the back pew.

Uncle Sam sat up in front with the choir dressed in his preacher clothes. When it came time for reading the lesson, someone else came up front to read. Louie listened carefully to the story from Acts about the Apostle Paul's ship caught in a storm.

Before very long, a wind of hurricane force, called a nor'easter, swept down from the island. The ship was caught by the storm and could not head into the wind. So we gave way to it and were driven along...

The *Tipsy*! The Bible story sounds just like the hurricane that Charlie's pa's ship was caught in, thought Louie!

When neither sun nor stars appeared for many days and the storm continued raging, we finally gave up all hope of being saved...

Louie wondered if Captain Missen and Ben had lost all hope, too. He listened intently as the reader read the part about what Paul said and did.

But now I urge you to keep up your courage, because not one of you will be lost, only the ship will be destroyed.[15]

After the reader finished reading, he sat back down in a pew and Uncle Sam stood up to preach.

All of us have just recently experienced a storm similar to the one described by the teller of this storm, probably Luke, Paul's companion. Remember, Paul was a prisoner and a centurion was taking him to Rome to make an appeal to the emperor, Caesar. They'd been on several different ships before setting sail from the island of Crete. Paul wanted the ship's captain to stay in Crete. He had a foreboding that they might run into bad weather and warned them that the cargo they were taking to Rome might be destroyed. It was this time of year when storms are most treacherous. They must have taken a vote, because the text says that the majority wanted to get going, throwing Paul's cautionary advice to the gentle south wind. Then they ran into the hurricane and lost all hope of being rescued.

We can also empathize with the fear and hopeless that the passengers and crew on the ship must have felt. If you have ever been caught in a boat in a storm or have had loved ones in a storm at sea, many of you may have experienced that same fear and hopelessness as Paul's shipmates did. Others may have gone out fishing or lobstering when bad weather threatened, because you needed to catch fish or lobsters to sell and could not miss a day of work.

"I have just left Mrs. Missen, her son Charlie, and daughter, Lucy. Captain Missen and his son, Ben, did not return from their fishing trip to the Grand Banks. They, too, had set out with the fishing fleet to make a living. The rest of the fleet returned but they are still lost at sea. A Life Saving Service boat has been sent out from Nova Scotia to look for them. But we must not give up hope because God is with them. We must be with the Missen family to support them through their hours of waiting."

After the sermon, Uncle Sam led the congregation in a prayer for the Missen family and the crew of the *Tipsy*.

"Get your gear, Louie," he said as he rushed to the back of the church and grabbed Louie's arm. "We've just enough time to get you to the dock to meet the steamer."

Rush they did and made it just as the steward was pulling up the gangway.

"Wait," Uncle Sam cried rushing toward the ship, his clergy robes flying in the wind behind him, as the crews were untying the ropes.

"I have a passenger for you!"

Louie threw his duffel and bedroll to the steward and leapt onto the deck from the wharf.

---

[15] Quotes chapter 27: vs 14-15, 20, 22.

CHAPTER 20

Homeward Bound

Slippery seals and dipping dolphins.

Louie watched them all from his bow perch. Seals dove from rock ledges and dolphins frolicked in the waves. The few passengers on board with Louie stayed on the decks. The *Dewline* rode smoothly in light winds.

Louie reminisced about the events of the past few days. He fingered the baseball in his pocket when he remembered the thrill of being near enough to Dougherty to have him autograph it. He recalled jostling and playing games with the other boys on the train. But his estrangement from Charlie contrasted with these happier moments and his stomach growled. That reminded him that he hadn't eaten since yesterday. He fingered the money left and went to find where the *Dewline* sold food.

Eating, reminiscing, and then sleeping passed the time until the *Dewline* pulled beside the familiar town wharf. Just as Louie was wondered how he was going to get out to Two Tree Island, he saw Captain Bowline and Tommy coming down the pathway from town.

Tommy ran to greet him with Sally and one of her puppies galloping along behind.

"How were the games?" Tommy said breathlessly, "Did you get any autographs?" Louie took out the baseball and showed it to him.

"Wow!" was all Tommy could say.

Captain Bowline shook his hand.

"Glad you're back safe and sound. Sam Hornblower sent me a wire ask'n me to meet ye and take ye back home. He told me about Charlie's broken arm and his pa and brother. Too bad. How'd it happen? The arm I mean."

Louie told them all about how they had sat on top of the fence during the first game and Charlie had fallen off and about getting Dougherty's autograph. He showed Tommy his Boston cap and, since he hadn't brought him anything, decided to give it to him, but he'd keep the baseball. Tommy pulled the cap down over his ears and hugged Louie.

Aussie, Ma, and Scout came down to the shore to greet Captain Bowline's dory when it arrived at the Two Tree Island landing. Louie and Tommy were sitting on the bow and Tommy had brought along Sally and one of the puppies.

Louie wasn't sure who was the happiest to see the other—Sally, to see Scout, Scout to see her sibling, or Ma to see Louie. Bedlam reigned as puppies tumbled over each other while Louie grabbed his duffel and bedroll and tried to get out of the dory. All collided. Louie, Tommy, and Aussie fell in a heap laughing with puppies crawling all over them.

Finally Aussie managed to disentangle himself enough to say goodbye. Louie opened his duffel and gave him the baseball cap he'd bought for him.

"Thanks for coming so I could go to the world championship games," he said handing him the cap. Aussie tried it on his tousled mop of red hair.

"'Preciate the thought, but think it's a wee bit small for me head. Like to blow right off me topper in a boat. Here you be keep'n it 'till I come back. Yer pup's been a'moaning for ye," he replied in his Scottish brogue. Then he climbed into the dory with Tommy, who had to bribe Sally and Scout's sister back into the boat with a treat.

"It's good to have you home, again." Ma put her arm around Louie.

"I'm glad to be back home, too," he said to Ma, but he wasn't sure he really wanted to be home. Not yet anyway. Not with Charlie still mad at him. Not when there were world championship games still going on.

Nevertheless, he told Ma all that had happened on the train ride, at the games, and at the campgrounds, but didn't tell her anything about Charlie.

"Did you and Charlie have a good time together?" Ma asked after they had returned from lighting the lamp wick.

"Yes, until he broke his arm and got into trouble. Then he found out when he got back home that his pa's ship was still lost at sea. Lucy and his ma were pretty upset."

Louie told her the whole story while they were eating supper.

"But Uncle Sam said at church on Sunday that we shouldn't give up hope and that we should pray for all the sailors and fishermen on the *Tipsy* to be rescued."

CHAPTER 21

Keeping Vigil

Praying did not stop the worrying.

All the next day Louie worried about Charlie. What if Charlie's pa and brother do not return? What if Charlie starts smoking again or gets drunk like his pa?

Louie went about his lighthouse chores with Scout at his heels—except when he was gathering eggs. The hens definitely did not like having Scout around. Neither did Betsy, who still mooed at Scout when Louie came to milk her. Louie thought Scout must have understood that Betsy wanted him to keep away because Scout sat and chewed on a piece of driftwood behind the cow shed while Louie milked.

Louie asked Ma when he went up to the house for dinner, "Did Betsy kick Scout while I was gone?"

"Yes—a good swift one. Made her yelp and she sure backed away."

She added, "Say, why don't we both write letters this afternoon. I'll write to Charlie's ma and you can write to Charlie. I expect Gus's mail boat to come by tomorrow. Then it's back to the school lessons."

Louie wrote the following with Scout curled up on his bed beside him:

> How you doin', Charlie? Been thinking much about you, your ma, and Lucy—praying, too, like Uncle Sam asked us. Are you still mad at me for telling Uncle Sam about your having that beer?
>
> Is your arm better? Did you get a new cast or do you still have the old one with all the names everyone signed at the campgrounds?
>
> Are you wearing your new baseball cap? I gave mine to Tommy—then Aussie gave me back the one I bought for him so I get to wear it when he's not here.
>
> Did Boston win any games in Pittsburgh? We don't have a wireless so I don't know what is happening. Hope they win. Please write and tell me what you hear.
>
> Here's cross hand'n you.
>
> —Louie

He sealed the letter and put a stamp on it and gave it to Gus the next day when he stopped at the island.

The rest of the week Louie helped Ma with the light beacon and, when he had completed all his chores for the day, he worked on his school lessons. Days melted into nights and nights into days. No news from Charlie and no news from the championship games in Pittsburgh.

"If the weather were any warmer and the wind not so brisk, I'd take the double-ender into town and find out what's going on," he said to Ma.

"Sometimes living on an island without any means of communicating with the outside world," agreed Ma, "can be pretty frustrating.

On Friday, the *Rainbow* arrived with Uncle Sam on board. Louie ran down to greet the dory as it pulled into the boat slip.

"What's happening?" Louie demanded while he was hooking up the dory to the slip. "Tell you and your ma when we get up to the house," was all Uncle Sam replied.

"But Charlie did get your letter and told me to tell you that he wasn't mad at you any more," he told Louie on the way back up to the house. Louie was relieved.

When they had all settled in the kitchen over cups of coffee and some muffins Ma had made, Uncle Sam reported the news.

"Charlie's arm is healing. The cast will come off in two weeks and it doesn't hurt as much. Still no news from the Life Saving Service so everyone's waiting and praying."

"And the games in Pittsburgh?" Louie asked.

"Just getting to that good news. Boston has tied up the games— three games apiece. They play again tomorrow. Here, I brought you the latest edition of the *Boston Globe* so you can read all about the games and what happened."

"I've decided to ask Mr. McAllister if I can take a leave for about ten days," Ma told Uncle Sam and Captain Bowline.

"I'd like to go and visit Mrs. Missen and see what I can do for them. Besides, I'm due for vacation time and Aussie said he'd come back and relieve me. He and Louie can man the light and tend to things while I'm gone."

"But I want to go, too," Louie interrupted.

"No, Louie. You've had your relief time. Now its my turn."

Uncle Sam nodded his head in agreement.

"I'll speak to Mr. McAllister and Aussie. Should be no problem."

Ma wrote a brief note to McAllister making the formal request. Then the two men headed back to town.

That night Louie wrote in the lighthouse logbook:

October 9, 1903: Weather turning cooler. Wind gusts from NE up to 20. Rainbow arrives. Boston has tied up the World Series.

—Louie Hollander

CHAPTER 22

Aussie

"Hello, laddy," the voice called.

Through the morning mist Louie couldn't see who belonged to the voice, but being called "laddy" made his back bristle. After all he wasn't a little kid any more. Then he recognized the Scottish brogue.

"Hi Aussie." Louie went down to meet the approaching dory.

"Reliev'n yer ma."

"I'll tell her you're here."

Just as Louie turned to start back to the house, he saw Ma coming toward them, duffel in hand.

Louie and Ma had discussed and made lists of all the items they needed during the long winter months ahead. He reminded her of her promise to buy him some new clothes because he'd outgrown or worn out almost all the clothes in his trunk. So she took out the tape measure and measured the length of Louie's arms and legs.

"And these shoes, they pinch my toes." So he and Ma looked at shoes and boots in a catalog and he picked out the ones he liked.

"Couldn't we get a Marconi wireless, too?" he begged. "Then I can keep up with the baseball news."

"First things first. Keeping vigil with Charlie's Ma. That comes first. Don't forget to do your lessons," she reminded Louie as she stepped into the waiting dory. She was off.

Louie walked with Aussie and Scout back to the house.

"Any news about the series?" was the first question from Louie.

"Should be play'n today. Field too wet for baseball yesterday."

Louie wished he could be at the Huntington Grounds ballpark or at least near a telegraph or telephone office so he could learn first hand about how his favorite team was doing. Instead, he was stuck here on this island wilderness with just Aussie. He sort of liked him when he'd met him before. Maybe they could be friends. Over supper he began to ask him questions so he could get to know him.

"How come you don't tend lighthouses full-time?"

"Well, now. Used to. Them thar's a tale worth tell'n. Raised as a young'n on an island like this 'till time to go to school. My ma wanted me to go to mainland to school. My pa put up a big fuss but Ma won out. I went to live with my Aunt Sally to git me school'n. Came back to stay on the island over holidays and help my pa with the lighthouse. Got bored—so's couldn't wait 'till school started. Now one foot likes being here, the other on the mainland."

Louie smiled. He felt the same way. He'd left one foot on the mainland, too.

"Are you married? Do you have any kids?"

"No to both questions, laddy. Came close once. But the lady wanted me to settle down and get a steady job—t'weren't right, I reckon. Now can I put off any more questions 'till tomorrow?"

Aussie settled his gear in the spare room while Louie went up to the loft to his lessons and reading. He opened his poetry book to a poem written by John Greenleaf Whittier called *Sea Dream*[16] and read the first stanza out loud:

We saw the slow tides go and come,
The curving surf-lines lightly drawn,
The gray rocks touched with tender bloom
Beneath the fresh-blown rose of dawn.

Scout perked up his ears and looked at Louie as if to say, go on. But Louie paused to think how well the poet described Two Tree Island. He read on to the third stanza:

On stormy eves from cliff and head
We saw the white spray tossed and spurned;
While over all, in gold and red,
Its face of fire the lighthouse turned.

Louie watched the beam of light careening across his bed and wondered if someone like him was manning a lighthouse near were the *Tipsy* had disappeared.

He picked up his pen and ink and wrote on a writing tablet:

"Through the seas the *Tipsy* tossed.
All wondered...was she lost?"

When his turn came to tend the light beacon, he wrote in the logbook:

October 13, 1903: Winds from NE. Archibald McKowen arrives
as relief lighthouse keeper. Last championship game of
World Series in Boston.
                                        —*Louie Hollander*

---

[16] <u>Complete Poetical Works of Whittier</u>, Cambridge Edition, 1892, 160.

CHAPTER 23

Sharing Lessons

Down in the dumps.

That's the way Louie felt when he woke up in the morning. Not knowing which team had won the First World Series; not knowing if Ma had arrived safely at Charlie's house; not knowing if the Life Saving Service had found the *Tipsy* or its crew. To top it off he heard the fog siren. Now gray mist would cover everything.

Scout snuggled up near Louie.

"At least I know you." Louie scratched behind Scout's ears. The puppy wagged his tail so hard the quilt fell off the bed. Louie pulled on his overalls and went to find Aussie in the kitchen.

"Morn'n, laddy. Fog came in whilst you was asleep'n." Aussie handed Louie a bowl of steaming porridge. "Best wear warm clothes under yer slickah. Cold snap settl'n in."

Louie finished his breakfast and pulled on the new wool sweater Ma had made him, then topped it off with his oilskin. He wondered if he'd need gloves when he milked Betsy but decided against wearing them because it would be too difficult to milk her with them on. Scout trailed at his heels keeping her distance from Betsy and from the hens who ruffled their feathers and hissed when Scout approached.

Louie took his turn manning the light beacon throughout the day. During his third shift while he was putting more kerosene in the wick reservoir something seemed not quite right. He stopped and listened to the sounds around him. He heard the familiar whir of the beacon turning and some seagulls calling but it was what he didn't hear that caught his attention.

"No fog siren. That's it. Quick Scout, we'll need to get the old bell going."

Louie finished lighting the wick and almost bumped into Aussie coming from the house as he came through the door at the bottom of the winding lighthouse tower steps.

"Get the bell a'clang'n. I'll see what's with that engine," Aussie called to Louie as he passed, then disappeared into the fog. Louie headed for the bell tower and hoped no ships were out there foundering. He uncleated the rope and started to pull on the crank to get the pulley going. Scout came up behind him and grabbed the end of the rope and pulled, too. Still the clacker hung loose. Something was stuck. Louie tried pulling again. Still stuck. Louie examined the rope and found a knot that kept the rope from releasing the bell clapper. He had to climb up the side of the tower to free it. Finally, he had the clapper hitting the side of the metal bell.

Clang, clang—every ten seconds. Louie remembered the drill. He had a hard time getting Scout to release the tension on the rope. Finally, persistence paid off and Scout was quick to pick up on the rhythm.

Aussie joined them an hour later.

"Got the machine work'n. Let's go inside where it's warm and I'll teach ye both a hauling shanty—so's next time ye both can work whilst sing'n."

As soon as they were both settled and had warmed themselves by the pot-bellied stove, Aussie took a fiddle from his duffel and sang:

"Now when I was a school boy I lived unto my teens
Now I am a trawling man, I sail the wintry seas.
I thought I'd like seafar'n life.
T'was all right 'till I found
t'was a damn site worse than slavery
when we got off the ground.
Haul boys haul,
Haul boys haul!
Heave away the capstan lads
and lets get up the trawl.
When the winds are blow'n,
when the ships are gently roll'n..
My Emma, my Emma won't you be true to me!
Now every night in winter, as reg'lar as a clock
Don we all sou'westers likewise your oilskin top.
Then up onto the capstans lads
then we'll heave away.
Now that's a cry in the middle of the night
as well as in the day.
Haul boys haul!…"[17]

After several rounds, Scout was hauling away on a piece of rope with Louie tugging on one end. Aussie played his fiddle, Louie sang, and Scout barked.

For the next hauling song, a song sung as sailors were hauling sails near the end of a voyage at sea, Louie fetched his harmonica and joined Aussie in singing and playing:

"O, the times are hard and the wages low,
Leave her, Johnny, leave her,
O, the times are hard and the wages low,
And it's time for us to leave her…
Oh, my old mother she wrote to me..,
'Oh my dear son, come back from the sea'…
It was rotten meat and weevilly bread..
'You'll eat or starve,' the old Man said…,
It's time for us to say goodbye…,
For the old pierhead is drawing nigh….
Leave her, Johnny, leave her,
Oh leave her, Johnny, leave her;
For the voyage is done and the winds don't blow,
And it's time for us to leave her."[18]

By midafternoon, Louie was so preoccupied learning new sea shanties from Aussie, he did not notice the fog had lifted. Now they could stop the fog siren and extinguish the lamp wick. The fresh wind from the northeast that had blown the fog away made it too cold to stay outside for long, so the two continued sharing lessons until dusk. Louie taught Aussie a few marble tricks and Aussie taught Louie some new knots to make the hours inside go by.

---

[17] Words from <u>Shanties and Songs of the Sea</u>, ARC Music Productions Inc. Ltd. 1998.

[18] Words from John Langstaff, chanteyman, <u>The Revels, Blow Ye Winds in the Morning</u>, 1992.

CHAPTER 24

News

Five days past.

Everyday Louie woke up thinking about Charlie, wondering who had won the World Series games, and when Ma would return. Maybe this could be the day they would hear some news. But no boats were sighted from Two Tree Island.

"Patience, laddy, we'll hear soon," was all Aussie said.

Louie thought he had been waiting patiently long enough. He had kept up with his lighthouse and household chores, trimming, lighting, and extinguishing wicks, washing the lighthouse tower windows, milking Betsy, and collecting eggs. He and Aussie hauled coal and washed clothes. Yet, as each day passed without even a glimpse of the *Rainbow* or the mail boat, anxiety floated like butterflies up into Louie's stomach.

On the morning of the sixth day, after inspecting the lighthouse beacon, Louie took the spyglass and scanned the sea. He nearly tripped over Scout when he ran down the winding lighthouse steps shouting, "Ship approaching!"

Before the boat had reached the wharf, Louie called out to the man at the helm, "What's the news?"

Then, he recognized Gus, the mailman, as he idled the motor nearing the wharf.

"Got some letters for ye," Gus called back.

Louie grabbed the bundle. Written on the outside of one of the envelopes in red bold letters were the words, *Boston Won!* Louie raced up the steps to the house waving the letter shouting, "Yippee!"

When he reached the house, he tore open the letter and read:

Dear Louie,

Bet you've been dying to know who won the championship games so the good news comes first. Our team had a 2-0 lead in the fifth inning then Ferris scored a single and brought LaChance home in the sixth to make it 3-0. The Pirates never did get in the game even though Phillip's pitching was first rate. The crowd went wild when we won.

Now for the bad news. Mrs. Missen has just received a wire from the Life Saving Service in Nova Scotia. They found Ben in a dory, near dead but still breathing. They've revived him enough to learn that the *Tipsy* broke up in the storm and all the fishermen and sailors on board perished, including Captain Missen. Ben's still in critical condition. We'll hear the whole story when he's well enough to come home...

Louie stopped reading and sat down on the nearest chair. All the adrenalin from the exciting baseball news rushed from his body and he felt only shock and anger. Hadn't Uncle Sam assured them that God would watch over the crew of the *Tipsy*? Why did God let it happen? Then he remembered, Ben was still alive, but barely. Would he live?

Then he felt Aussie's arm on his shoulder.

"Bad eh?" he queried.

"Not all bad—some good, some bad."

Louie read the part he had just finished reading out loud to Aussie then continued reading the rest of the letter.

...In any case, your ma wanted me to see if Aussie could stay for while longer so you can come for the memorial service for Captain Missen and the rest of the crew of the *Tipsy*. It's being planned for this Saturday. If you came on Friday, we can meet your train.

—Uncle Sam

"Could you?" Louie asked Aussie.

"Sure, laddy. Scout and I will manage. And we'll ask the good Lord to bring Ben through, too."

October 19, 1903. Wind SW 15.Gusts up to 25. Mail boat arrives. Tipsy lost at sea.

—Louie Hollander

CHAPTER 25

Consoling

"B est leave when ye can."

Aussie advised the next day. *What he meant to add,* Louie thought, *was weather permitting and to board the next boat arriving that made it to the island from the mainland.* Although the weather stayed cold and windy, Gus did return in the mail boat on Thursday and had room to take Louie to the mainland.

Louie stayed with the Bowlines overnight and took the local train on Friday. Ma met him at the train station and threw her arms around him. Neither of them talked for a while—just hugged each other. Louie felt a little less sad.

"Thought we'd shop first for some dress up clothes to wear to the funeral service," she said after she pulled away and dabbed at a tear with a handkerchief. She stopped the carriage at a local dry goods store that featured in its window, "Men's and Boys Clothing—All Sizes." Louie tried on several different jackets and selected a black one.

"Just make sure there's room to let the hem down on the cuffs of this jacket because my boy's growing so fast," Ma told the clerk. The clerk showed her the extra material in the sleeve cuffs. Next she purchased a white shirt with a high collar, a string tie, and a pair of long dark gray trousers. Louie tried them all on and admired himself in the mirror the clerk provided. Finally he didn't look like a little kid anymore with those awful knickers.

Next Louie went with Ma to Charlie's house where the town's folk had gathered to pay their respects. Louie was shocked to see Charlie. He was sitting by himself in a corner while his sister, Lucy, served food to the visitors. Mrs. Missen greeted Louie.

"I'm glad you came, Louie. Charlie needs you."

Louie went over to where Charlie was sitting by himself. His face was drawn and there were dark circles under his eyes as if someone had given him a black eye. His arm was still in a cast. It was no longer white but an ashen gray, like the color of Charlie's face.

Louie put his hand on Charlie's good arm and said.

"Sorry about your pa. Guess you wish all these people would just go away and leave you alone."

Charlie nodded.

"Let's go somewhere and talk." Louie put his arm through Charlie's and they maneuvered their way through the crowd of people and out the door. Still linking his arm with Charlie's, Louie guided him down to the pier. They sat dangling their legs over the water. Neither of them spoke for what seemed to Louie like a long time. Then Louie said,

"When my pa died, you came to see me, remember?"

Charlie nodded again.

"I was really upset. I thought if I'd only gotten to Pa sooner, he might not have died."

"It's my fault!" Charlie blurted out.

"You didn't cause the hurricane. You couldn't walk on water or fly in the air to save him or the ship."

"But I wished him dead!" Charlie buried his head in his hands. His shoulders shook as he sobbed.

"I hated him. He beat Ma and threw things around the house when he was drunk. Ben was his favorite. It was only when I got into trouble at school that he paid any attention to me—then it was to tan my hide."

Charlie flailed his cast and his free arm in the air. Louie had to grab him around the waist because it seemed like he was going to fly off the pier into the water.

Louie felt a firm grip on his shoulder and a hand reached over to help restrain Charlie from falling.

"Don't need another drowning today," Uncle Sam's voice said. "Let's walk and talk for a while."

Uncle Sam put his arm around both boys and together they walked into town to the ice cream parlor. While they walked Charlie repeated what he had told Louie, that he had caused his pa and the rest of the men on the ship to drown because he had wished him dead.

"You weren't responsible for your pa's drowning and you weren't responsible for the way he acted when he was drunk. Nothing you said or did could have changed either," he assured Charlie.

"It's OK to be angry—even to be angry at God for not stopping the ship from breaking up at sea with all the loss of lives—but it's not OK to blame yourself."

While sipping their Brown Cows[19], Uncle Sam and Charlie told Louie all they had heard about the World Series games in Pittsburgh and Boston. Louie and Ma stayed with Charlie and his family at the Missens' house that night and helped them get ready for the funeral service.

---

[19] Root beer with ice cream floating in it.

CHAPTER 26

Remembering the Drowned

People packed the church.

Louie was glad they had gotten there early to get a seat. *Packed in like sardines*, he thought, as he sat down next to Ma in a pew behind Charlie and his family. All the families of the crew of the *Tipsy* sat in the first pews. Other fishermen from the fleet either sat in special seats in the sanctuary or stood along the walls.

Preacher Sam came in and stood at the door of the church and announced.

"We are here gathered to honor the brave men on the *Tipsy*, who lost their lives at sea. We've placed a lighted candle on the altar to represent each seaman's life. We know from the words of Jesus in the Bible that their souls will live on with him in Heaven. For he said, 'I am the resurrection and the life; whosoever believes in me, even though he has died, shall live; and whosoever lives and believes in me shall never die.' And so we remind ourselves by singing the next hymn:"[20]

Voices sang in unison:

"Eternal Father, strong to save,
whose arm hath bound the restless wave,
Who bidd'st the mighty ocean deep,
its own appointed limits keep:
O hear us when we cry to thee for
those in peril on the sea.....
O Trinity of love and power,
thy children shield in danger's hour;
From rock and tempest, fire and foe,
protect them wheresoe'er they go;
Thus evermore shall rise to thee glad hymns of
praise from land and sea."

A family member and a fisherman got up to give a eulogy for each of the fisherman who had gone down with the *Tipsy*. Captain Missen's eulogy came last. Two of the fishermen came up to the lectern to speak about Charlie's pa. Charlie leaned back to whisper in Louie's ear, "They're my pa's buddies that drank with him at the Ocean View Bar."

"Me and me friend here, don't rightly know what we can say 'bout Benji, so, since we enjoyed sing'n together, thought we'd sing 'bout him using the words of the whal'n song. Ye all join in the chorus."

One of the fisherman took out his harmonica and started them off with the refrain.

"Blow ye winds in the morning,
Blow, ye winds, high-ho!
Clear away the running gear,
And blow, boys, blow!"[21]

The two sailors sang the verses. The congregation belted out the chorus after each verse.

(1) "Tis advertised in Boston, New York, and Buffalo,
A handful brave Americans a-fishing for to go.

(2) When they was off to sea, my boys, the winds come on to blow;
One half the watch was sick on deck, the other half below.

(3) They need to fill their ship with fish and they don't head for land.
They bent their sails, my boys, and sailed for Grand Banks sand.

(4) With fish in hold, their ship heaved to, a'waiting for the storm to pass.
Some took to boats to ride out the waves. Capt'n Missen stayed 'till last."

All eyes turned to the Missen family to see who would speak next for Captain Missen. Charlie got out of his seat and slowly made his way to the lectern. Louie wondered what he would say after yesterday. He wondered if he could or should tell the truth about his pa.

Charlie took a piece of paper out of his pocket and read:

Ma, Lucy, and I want to thank you for bringing us food and keep'n yer vigil with us since we learn'd about the *Tipsy* being lost and all. As for saying something about Pa, I wish Ben were here 'cause he was with Pa and can tell you all about what happened during that hurricane. Ben's still in the hospital. Guess you could say that Ben being still alive is the miracle we've been praying for. Me be'n the next oldest son was asked to say something about Pa.

Charlie paused and looked over at Louie. Louie mouthed, "It's OK." Then Charlie turned and looked at Uncle Sam who winked at him. Charlie turned back to the paper he'd been reading from, crumbled it, and threw it on the floor.

I didn't' really know Pa like most boys know'd their pa. When I was little, I can remember him carefully taking the fishhook out of my hand when it got caught there the day he took me with him fish'n. But that was the last time I went fish'n with him. Usually he was out fish'n on the *Tipsy*.

Charlie looked over at the other fishermen around the church and continued,

"Guess you know'd him better than me 'cause he spent most of the time when he wasn't fish'n at the Ocean View with you."

The men squirmed in their seats. Wives turned and glared at their husbands. Charlie paused, then continued,

"Most of the time when Pa was home he was mean to us. That's all I got to say about my pa."

Uncle Sam came over and put his arm around Charlie's shoulders, then walked with him back to his seat in the pew. Mrs. Missen shook her finger at Charlie when he sat down in his seat next to her. Lucy just cried. Louie leaned over and whispered in Charlie's ear, "You told it like it was—that's honest."

After the service, Louie asked Ma if Charlie could come stay with them on Two Tree Island when Mrs. Missen left to go be with Ben.

"All arranged," Ma replied.

---

[20] William Whiting, 1861.

[21] The Revels, <u>Blow Ye Winds in the Morning</u>: track 13.

CHAPTER 27

Keepers Return

Louie helped Charlie pack his gear.

Charlie insisted on bringing his rifle to the island with him. Louie didn't like the idea.

"Aw com'on," Charlie said, "I'm tak'n rifle practice at school. Besides we might want to shoot at a few sea gulls."

"No sea gulls!" Louie shouted in alarm. "Besides, you can't shoot with your arm in a cast."

"Just teas'n, Louie. My cast comes off this afternoon, then I can move my arm again. Besides I'll just practice shoot'n at rocks."

With that, Louie finally relented to Charlie's bringing the rifle. Ma agreed as long as it was just target practice.

Louie went with Charlie to the hospital to have his cast cut off.

"Are you his friend?" the doctor asked Louie.

"Yep. But sometimes he gets mad at me."

"Even if he gets mad at you, keep after him to keep his arm in this sling and make sure he exercises it once a day."

Charlie and Mrs. Missen left with Louie and Ma the next day by train. Mrs. Missen planned to go to the hospital in Nova Scotia where Ben recuperated. Rough seas prevented Louie, Charlie, and Ma from going to Two Tree Island the day they arrived in town so they had to stay overnight with the Bowlines. That gave Ma time to shop for everything on her list at Jake's store while Louie and Charlie took Tommy clamming at low tide.

When the weather cleared, Captain Bowline ferried the three of them with all their satchels and boxes of groceries over to Two Tree Island on the *Rainbow*.

Aussie greeted them and said to Ma, "You'll find everything shipshape. Weather and equipment cooperated."

Ma shook his hand.

"Really appreciated your willingness to relieve me for a spell. We were glad to be with the Missens at this time and Charlie has come back to visit."

"Glad to help—anytime," Aussie said to Ma as he collected his gear to return in the *Rainbow* with Captain Bowline.

"I'll be miss'n Scout. She and I got to be real pals."

Aussie patted Scout's head and Scout jumped up and licked his face.

Louie reached over and drew Scout back. After all Scout was his pet—not Aussie's. Resentment crawled up his spine. He liked Aussie, but he didn't like Scout taking to anyone else. She was his pet. He picked her up and held her close.

After helping Ma up to the house with their food and household supplies, Louie and Charlie threw some sticks for Scout to fetch. Louie had also brought an old ball from Tommy's house and he taught Scout to catch it when he threw it up in the air.

That night Louie read Aussie's log entries. Nothing much had happened while they were away except a little wind. No foggy days. *Must have been Indian summer weather*, Louie thought. Aussie had noted a few ships passing the lighthouse, but that was all. Louie added his notes for that day after lighting the lamp wick and then joined Charlie, who had already gone to bed:

October 26, 2005. Winds SSE 15-20. Hollander keepers
return from funeral of Tipsy crew. Charlie Missen comes to
visit.

—Louie Hollander

CHAPTER 28

Foul Play

Charlie screamed.

"What's wrong?" Louie woke up alarmed. The light from the lamp beacon careened through their loft bedroom.

"Just a bad dream, I guess." Charlie sat up in bed.

"I was on the *Tipsy* when a big wave came over and I saw Pa being washed overboard. I tried to go to him but my feet were glued to the deck. I called for help but the wind drowned out my calls." Sweat broke out on Charlie's brow.

Louie reached over and held Charlie's free hand.

"You weren't there, Charlie, and you couldn't save him."

Charlie rolled over on his mending arm.

"Ouch!"

Louie didn't get much sleep the rest of that night because Charlie moaned, tossed, and turned. When the sun came through the dormer window, Louie dragged himself out of bed to do his lighthouse chores. Charlie now slept soundly.

"Let him sleep," Ma said at breakfast. "He's had to be the man in the family for the past few weeks. We need to give him space to rest and deal with his pa's death the best way he can."

After morning chores, Louie tiptoed up the loft steps. Charlie was still a sleep, so he took a geometry book outside under the two trees to catch up on his lessons. But it was hard to concentrate. With the book and pad of paper open beside him he dosed off to the "kuk kukking" of the seagulls and the "lap lapping" of the waves.

He woke up with a start when he felt someone tapping on his shoulder. It was Charlie with Scout. Charlie had his rifle under his good arm.

"Time for rifle practice," he said. "Want to learn? This here's an old military bolt rifle, uses .223 caliber ammo."

Louie shook his head. "No, thanks. I don't like guns. But I'll have to hold Scout's ears or the noise will hurt them."

Charlie made a target by building a pile of pebbles on top of larger rock that hung over the edge of cliff. Charlie held the rifle butt with his mending arm and sighted through the barrel releasing the bolt with his good arm.

"Bang! Bang!" the sound made both Scout and Louie jump. The pile of pebbles broke apart and scattered. Louie kept his distance and held his hands as tightly as he could over Scout's ears.

Just then a flock of geese heading south for the winter came honking overhead.

Charlie moved his rifle and pointed toward the V shaped formation.

"No!" Louie screamed. "Don't shoot! You promised."

Charlie kept his rifle high and put his finger on the bolt as the geese formation drew closer.

"Bang!" One of the geese fell. Charlie aimed again.

"Don't Charlie!" Louie shouted again, "You promised not to shoot birds!"

Louie released his hold on Scout and leapt forward. He tried to grab the rifle out of Charlie's hands. They wrestled. Scout pulled on Charlie's foot and Charlie went over, releasing, the bolt trigger as he fell. The bullet ricocheted off a rock and came back toward them.

"Duck!" Charlie screamed.

Louie let go of Charlie and reached out to grab Scout but he was too late. Scout leapt into the air and yipped. Louie clutched his shoulder and bent over double.

"Oh no!" Charlie dropped the rifle and with horror looked over at Louie.

Ma came running toward them, wiping her hands on her apron as she came.

"What happened?"

"Louie's hurt—maybe Scout—the bullet..."

Ma reached Louie's side and knelt down beside Louie who by this time was writhing in pain. What she saw made her gasp. Louie had a deep gash in his shoulder and it was bleeding badly. She tore her apron in pieces and wrapped it tightly around the wound. Scout licked Louie's face. Louie started moaning and looked at Scout.

"The bullet missed him, but not you. I'm sorry." Charlie said and started crying.

Ma glared at Charlie.

"You can make your apologies later young man. You're just lucky no one was killed here. Now I need you to help Louie back up to the house and send out an SOS signal."

Ma held the improvised bandage around Louie's wound while Charlie put his arm around Louie to help him back up to the house. Scout followed. Ma put a blanket on the kitchen table and laid Louie on top.

"Get the medicine chest—it's over there," Ma told Charlie. She took some morphine out of the chest and gave it to Louie. Then she examined the wound to see if the bullet was lodged anywhere and not finding it she swabbed the wound with iodine and bandaged it as best she could. Then she turned to Charlie.

"Don't just stand there looking sheepish. Get that SOS flag up the flagpole and send out a signal from the tower. Start flashing the light beacon."

CHAPTER 29

Shame

Gus saw the signal from his mail boat.
He turned his boat around and made straight for the town dock, then ran to Mr. McAllister's office. Mr. McAllister went to find Nurse Figgins, and then down to the town wharf to see if the lighthouse tender was in port. She wasn't, but he asked Captain Bowline if he would take them to the island on the *Rainbow*. Captain Bowline was swabbing[22] the decks of the *Rainbow*.

"Better git Doc Bowen. Never can tell with young'ns," he cautioned.

In two hours, the *Rainbow* had anchored off Two Tree Island. Doc jumped out of the dory first carrying his black bag. Nurse Figgins followed.

Ma gave them both a running account as she rushed them up to the house.

> "Louie's hurt.
> Gash in shoulder.
> Hit by bullet.
> Don't know if bullet still in there.

Bandaged him best I could.
Gave him morphine for pain."

"Can't find any bullet," Doc Bowen reassured her after he examined Louie's shoulder, "but he will need some stitches. Nurse Figgins, please give him some morphine while I sew him up." Louie moaned for a while, then he was out.

Charlie stopped flashing the beacon when the dory pulled up. But he didn't come into the house. Instead he went out to the place where he'd set up the target practice. When he returned, he stood in the doorway watching Doc finishing stitching up Louie's shoulder.

"This will heal but he'll need to keep his shoulder immobile. May hurt for a while." Doc closed his black bag and wrote down some instructions for Ma.

Charlie, who was still standing in the doorway, said quietly, "I found the bullet. It was lodged in between two rocks."

"Now I'll deal with you, young man." Nurse Figgins turned and glared at Charlie. Ma went over to Charlie and guided him over to sit in the nearest chair.

"Guns are not play things. They kill. What were you do'n with that thing anyway?" Nurse Figgins demanded.

"I was…just practic'n shooting rocks. Then I saw the geese flying overhead and I killed one of them." He stopped talking.

"You promised Louie you wouldn't shoot any birds," Ma shouted at Charlie. "You just broke that promise and almost killed your best friend and my only son." She spat out the words. "If you were any younger I'd give you a good thrashing!"

Charlie hung his head and started sobbing. "I'm–m–m sorry," he mumbled in between sobs.

Ma went back to tend to Louie who was now waking up. Doc, Mr. McAllister, and Captain Bowline carried Louie up to his loft bed. When Louie passed Charlie, he said in a slow voice,

"I… tried… to stop… you… from killing… more birds… you didn't…listen. "

Then he looked down at Ma who was coming up the stairs.

"Ma…just…an…accident."

"An accident waiting to happen," Mr. McAllister added. He glared once more at Charlie, who stood at the bottom of the stairs with one hand in his pocket.

"I think I'd best take that rifle back with me for safe keep'n. Next time you want to practice shooting, you can come up to town and we'll go to a shooting range and learn some dos and don'ts about using guns. Meanwhile, son, you best help Mrs. Hollander until Louie's shoulder heals."

Charlie bent his head and held the arm that was in the sling.

Doc Bowen saw him wince and said, "Here let me take a look at that arm. Did you hurt it, too?"

Charlie explained that he had broken his arm earlier and that the cast had just come off.

After examining Charlie's arm, Doc Bowen said, "Least you didn't break it again, but that bone's still mending and there seem to be some new bruises. Best keep it immobile for a day or so."

Mr. McAllister took the rifle and the bullets with him to the waiting dory. Doc Bowen said he'd come back to take the stitches out and to see how Louie and Charlie were doing.

"Keep putting fresh dressings on the wound," he told Ma, "and give Louie some morphine every four hours until tomorrow if he needs it."

Ma went down with the men and Nurse Figgins to the landing area to see them all off. While she was gone, Charlie went up to the loft, but Louie was sound asleep so he came back down again. Ma was back and cleaning up the kitchen.

"I'm sorry, Ma'am. I bet you wish you could send me home but I got no place to go. I can't do anything right, that's what Pa used to yell at me. I'm just a rotten kid."

Ma sighed and came over to Charlie and put her hand on his shoulder.

"No. You're not a rotten kid and you can do things right. You just broke a promise to Louie and me and that's wrong. What happened with the bullet was an accident. But you're not an accident. God doesn't make junk. He makes each individual special and you have special talents. You're also Louie's friend and we both love you."

---

[22] Scrubbing the decks with a mop.

CHAPTER 30

Healing

Louie's shoulder throbbed.

He gritted his teeth and held on to the sides of the mattress when the waves of pain came. Scout crawled in beside him and licked Louie's face. Ma put some pillows behind his head to take the pressure off the shoulder. It helped some but the morphine helped more. He slept on and off that night.

Charlie went with Ma to help her light the lamp wick. He could do that lighthouse chore with his free hand. Ma opened a can of sardines to go with biscuits and milk for supper. Louie didn't feel much like eating. But Charlie found that he was hungry. They had all missed eating dinner earlier because of tending to Louie.

Louie found that after the first twenty-four hours the pain in his shoulder hurt less and he stopped taking the morphine. He could sit up, read, or play cards with Charlie, although it still hurt to move around much. They talked for hours about their fathers.

Charlie told Louie that during his pa's drunken rages, he and Ben had intervened to try and protect his ma when his pa started hitting her. Charlie said he would try to pull his ma away while Ben wrestled with their pa. As he was telling the story, Charlie threw a pillow down on the floor and stomped on it with his feet.

"It gets me all riled up just remember'n." He kept stomping until Ma came up to the loft to see what was going on.

Later, he told Louie how Lucy usually cowered in a corner and cried. Ben often went to the Ocean View to try to get their pa to come home before he got too drunk. But his pa would shoo Ben away.

"I'm glad my pa wasn't like that," Louie said. "Since I was a little baby, he wanted me by his side. Ma said he even took me in a basket up to the lighthouse tower when he was on watch. I felt so empty when he died. Then I met Uncle Sam. Sometimes he reminds me of my pa."

"I like him, too. He's like a pa should be."

"Suppose he'll marry one of our mas?" Louie queried.

"Naw," replied Charlie, "He's not the marr'n kind."

"Maybe, maybe not," Louie added. He sort of wished Uncle Sam would marry his ma though. Then again, he and Ma wouldn't be a lighthouse keeping team anymore. She would have to be a preacher's wife. *Life would sure be different*, Louie thought.

When the fog set in again, Charlie helped Ma with the light beacon. Scout sniffed the air and went right to the fog bell and began to tug on the rope.

"Don't need you yet, girl," Charlie told her, "as long as the fog siren works."

He took her up to the loft to be stay with Louie.

The *Rainbow* returned when the fog lifted with Doc Bowen and Nurse Figgins.

"Making much progress here," he said after examining Louie's shoulder and Charlie's arm.

"That sling can come off you soon, Charlie, then Louie can wear it for a while to keep the shoulder still while it heals." He took the stitches out and put some salve on the wounded area.

"Almost forgot," Captain Bowline said as Doc and Nurse Figgins boarded the dory to take them out to the *Rainbow*, "this letter came for you, Charlie. Telegram, too, for yer Ma." He handed the telegram to Ma and the letter to Charlie.

Ma read the telegram:

Ben's wounds are healing. Stop. Coming home next week. Stop. Will fetch Charlie en route. Stop. Depending on weather. Stop.
—Mary Ann Missen

"Charlie, what's in your letter?" Ma asked when they got back up to the house.

"It's in Ma's handwrit'n but looks like it's from Ben." He sat down at the kitchen table to read the letter. Then took it upstairs to read it out loud to Louie.

Dear Brother,

You may wonder why I'm not writing this but I can't. My hands are still bandaged. Got badly frostbitten and still swollen. My feet, too.

Wanted you to be the first to know, after I told Ma, what happened to Pa, the crew, and me.

Don't rightly know how I survived. The doctors here and the Life Saving Crew that rescued me said it was a miracle. I can believe it because I thought I was already in Heaven when I woke up here with Ma beside me.

Charlie stopped reading and breathed a sigh of relief. He was glad to know that Ben didn't go to Heaven. He continued reading.

When the storm came up, I was in one of the dories out trawling for cod. There were three of us. We had let out the tub trawl and were waiting for the fish to bite to hawl the line in. It was windy with some following seas—then these big black clouds blocked out the sun and the wind changed direction on us. All of a sudden the waves were coming at us. I was row'n at the time and turned her around to head into the wind—but we also headed into the tub and trawl line. I saw the tub coming and tried to skirt around her but one of the hooks caught the man pay' n out the line and pulled him overboard. I shouted at the next sailor to cut the line—which he did—none too soon 'cause the line was about to hook the bottom of the boat. We tried to get to the fisherman who had gone overboard but the barrel hit him first and down he went.

"Hully Gee," Louie said, "must have been awful for Ben to see that man drown." Charlie continued reading Ben's story.

We saw an outline of a ship in the distance floundering around and listing to starboard and made for her over the waves. My mate, Frank, had to bail when the waves washed over us—but we stayed afloat. When we neared the *Tipsy*, men were falling off the spars with all the sails torn. We fished two of them out of the ocean and watched helplessly as the *Tipsy* broke up and went under. Pa was still at the wheel when she went down.

Charlie stopped reading. Louie looked over at his friend. Charlie swallowed hard and then read on.

The waves were huge. But somehow we managed to stay afloat. The two sailors who had been in the ocean lay in the bottom of the boat shivering. Frank and I kept bailing as fast as the water came in. But it wasn't fast enough. The two sailors we'd fished out of the ocean died.

As soon as the storm had blown over Frank and I took turns rowing. We didn't know where—all we saw was gray heaving water all around us. We had been able to catch some rainwater in the bait barrel, after dumping out the bait. Some of the trawl

line with the hooks was still in the dory, so we fished with that and ate the fish raw.

"Ugh!" Louie interrupted.

After two days, the seas grew calmer but we didn't know where we were. Then Frank became delirious. He was no good to row so I took to the oars. My hands were so cold that they froze around them. I tied myself to the mid seat and kept on rowing, although eventually I must have blacked out. When the Life Saving Ship found me, they say I was barely breathing. Frank was dead. They took me on board with my hands still curled around the oars and thawed out my hands enough until they could remove the oars.

I was running a high fever and in a coma for many days. The docs weren't sure I would come to.

Charlie paused again, "I wonder if he'll be able to keep his hands. Sometimes limbs that get frozen have to be cut off..." his voice faltered, but he finished reading the letter.

Ma told me about the memorial service and all the prayers 'aforehand. The Lord must have meant me to live 'cause I'm still here. Docs say I might be well enough to come home next week sometime. Since I still can't walk, Life Saving Crew says they'll ferry me home on their ship, weather permitt'n and will stop at Two Tree Island to fetch you.

—Ma writ'n for Ben

Charlie put down the letter and covered his face with his hands and sobbed. Tears of joy and sadness mingled and dropped on the letter lying on his lap. Louie picked up a pencil and pad of paper and began to write the response to Miss Gilbert's question.

To order additional copies of

Weathering the STORMS

Have your credit card ready and call:

1-877-421-READ (7323)

or please visit our web site at
www.pleasantword.com

Also available at:
www.amazon.com
and
www.barnesandnoble.com

CPSIA information can be obtained at www.ICGtesting.com
Printed in the USA
LVOW060032280512

283478LV00002B/42/A